The Ice Giant

Handersen Publishing, LLC
Lincoln, Nebraska

The Ice Giant

Manufactured in the United States of America.

Summary: Elika wants nothing to do with adventure and mythical creatures. But when she starts to hear the cries of a lonely giant, her only option is to follow them. On the glaciers of Iceland, she will meet her own giant, the Ice Giant.

Library of Congress Control Number: 2018963514
Handersen Publishing, LLC, Lincoln, Nebraska

Paperback ISBN-13: 978-1-947854-46-8
Hardback ISBN-13: 978-1-947854-47-5
eBook ISBN-13: 978-1-947854-48-2

Publisher Website: www.handersenpublishing.com
Publisher Email: editors@handersenpublishing.com

The Ice Giant

Giulietta M. Spudich

Handersen Publishing, LLC
Lincoln, Nebraska

Chapter
One

A cozy house with a blue door stood at the top of a hill in the suburbs of Hartsdale, New York. It was just perfect for a family of three. Sammy, a thirty-five-year-old scientist, lived there with his Icelandic wife Dorotea, also a scientist. Their daughter Elika, who had just turned thirteen, was in her bedroom getting ready for dinner.

Elika loved being in her room, which had a slanted ceiling that came to a point in the middle. It was just under their triangle-shaped roof. But tonight she was not in a happy place.

Elika passed a comb through her straight, dark hair and scowled.

Normally, Friday was her favorite day. It was the last day of the school week and the beginning of the weekend. But tonight, she wished it wasn't

Friday. Dad's sister, Aunt Caroline, was coming to dinner to celebrate Elika's birthday.

Really, a better birthday gift would be to not come to dinner.

She hated Aunt Caroline.

Elika winced as her comb caught a tangle.

The problem was, her aunt was extremely weird.

She wasn't the only one who was weird. It ran in her family. Her dad was mostly OK. But her mom was a little weird. And Elika herself...

She studied her face in the mirror. She didn't look like anyone else she knew. Her straight black hair was from her mom, who had been born to one of the few Chinese families in Iceland. That much was fine. Normal enough.

But Elika's almond-shaped green eyes turned yellow in certain lights. No one could say where Elika's eyes came from, or her high cheekbones.

Elika wished she had her dad's brown eyes, which were always brown in all lights and never turned yellow.

She had actually been called zombie-girl at school because of her eyes.

Also, her parents' favorite band was a woman called Bjork.

"What a weird name," Elika said to her reflection.

"Of course, it's no weirder than Elika," she said, once she had thought about it.

She sighed and finished combing her hair. Elika took comfort in the fact that however strange her immediate family was, it was nothing compared to Aunt Caroline.

Aunt Caroline looked normal enough. She had brown, curly hair and dark eyes like Elika's Dad. Her clothes were pretty normal—jeans, t-shirts, blouses and sweaters. To look at her, you'd never know that Aunt Caroline was best friends with a giant.

Seriously. A giant in the Himalayan mountains, in Nepal. Aunt Caroline went there every chance she could get.

Elika had seen pictures of the thing. It was all covered with hair.

She knew the story of how Aunt Caroline found the Amber Giant and woke him up from a thousand-year sleep and everything. Her dad had read her the story about a million times. Aunt Caroline had written it for him when they were kids. That only proved to Elika that Aunt Caroline had always been weird.

Elika wasn't allowed to talk about the Amber Giant outside her family. As if she would. Everyone at school thought she was strange enough.

Why Aunt Caroline couldn't be best friends with a human instead of a giant, Elika didn't know.

Giants weren't normal friends to have.

"Elika!" her mom called up the stairs. "Caroline just parked in the driveway. Come down for your birthday dinner!"

Elika took a deep breath. It wasn't really her birthday dinner. She had already celebrated with her parents on Wednesday night, her actual birthday. They had pizza and watched a fun movie.

Just because Aunt Caroline wanted to celebrate Elika's birthday, she had to have another, much less fun birthday dinner.

Elika sighed again. She just had to get through dinner. She hoped Aunt Caroline wouldn't go on an on with her stories about giants. But based on past experience, she probably would.

There was nothing left to do but put on a smile and try to make the best of it, as her grandma used to say. Elika had promised her parents she would be nice to Aunt Caroline. She had even written it on her hand.

"Be nice to Aunt Caroline," Elika read aloud.

Elika believed strongly in promises.

Her grandma used to say that a promise was written in the heart.

So Elika had to be nice. She just hoped Aunt Caroline wouldn't tell too many giant jokes. Then, promise or not, she would truly scowl.

Chapter Two

On Saturday morning, the sun streamed through Elika's window, brightening up her room. She spread her crystal collection out on the bedspread. They were so pretty in the sun.

Elika liked to touch each one and say its name.

"Hematite, Green Opal, Amethyst, Fire and Ice Quartz," Elika recited.

She added a new, clear quartz crystal from Aunt Caroline. Though the dinner with Aunt Caroline was weird, with all the stories about her giant helping lost hikers in the mountains, at least Elika got a cool crystal out of it.

"Himalayan Quartz," Elika said as she placed it at the end of the line of stones. She had washed it in case that hairy giant had touched it or something. Now it shone in the sun, all clean.

Her hand was also clean. She had washed the promise off. She didn't have to try to be nice to Aunt Caroline now.

Elika held her favorite crystal in her clean palm. The Green Opal was beautiful, and had green, brown and white colors in it. It was so smooth. There was something nice about it, something almost French.

Elika loved all things French.

Her second favorite crystal was the Fire and Ice Quartz. Mom brought that one back from Iceland.

Though Elika didn't like Iceland, of course. It was a weird country with a weird language. When you came right down to it, Elika didn't want to be half-Icelandic. If she had a choice, she would be part French.

The French were so cool. They invented things like croissants. A boy named Henry in school was from France. Their family just moved here. He said his name in a cool way, like *Ahn-ree* or something, with an awesome accent.

That's why, when her mom offered her lessons in Icelandic for her birthday, Elika asked for French lessons instead.

Mom wanted her to learn Icelandic, but no one spoke Icelandic except, of course, people in Iceland. People spoke French all over the world.

"They speak French in Canada, in France, in Belgium," Elika had explained to her mom.

"But you're half Icelandic," her mom said. "Don't you want to learn the language of your people?"

"You said everyone in Iceland speaks English," Elika had replied. "So I am speaking the language of my people, I guess."

Mom looked sad at first. But then she shrugged and said, "We'll see what we can do."

Her parents gave her an online French language course for her birthday. And for their summer vacation, they were going to Niagara Falls and crossing over into Canada.

Elika was thrilled that she was going to a cool place like Niagara Falls. She heard there were signs written in French in Canada. Maybe they had good croissants there too.

Also, she could ask Henry about French words, now that she was learning the language. She liked having Henry as a friend. He never talked about anything like giants. He was normal.

Elika studied the Fire and Ice crystal that Mom had gotten in Iceland. It was pretty in a different way to the Green Opal. It looked broken inside, like cracked ice, but it was smooth in her hand.

The smell of pancakes reached her nose. Her mom was making Dad's favorite breakfast. Elika felt a pang of hunger. She loved pancakes too.

This was going to be a good day. Not only were they going to have pancakes for breakfast, they were going on a picnic in the afternoon. It was the first sunny weekend since the rainy beginning of spring.

They would take a basket of sandwiches and a frisbee to the park and hang out by the lake. Elika loved being by the water. Her parents said it was because she was half Icelandic, but Elika didn't think so. Anyone would like being by the lake.

A gleam of light caught her eye. The Fire and Ice crystal in her hand caught the sun in a way that made it shine.

The smell of pancakes made her stomach

rumble. Elika placed the crystal next to the others on her bed.

That was weird. It was shining a lot brighter than the other crystals, which were also in the sun.

Elika shrugged. It probably didn't mean anything. She put the crystal collection in her desk drawer, and hopped out of the room to go downstairs for breakfast.

After breakfast, Elika did her homework. She finished just in time for the picnic, which was awesome. She and her dad played Frisbee while her mom cheered them on. Then they had ice cream. It was so much fun, Elika didn't even mind when her mom played Bjork music on the car ride home. The songs even seemed kind of pretty, if Elika listened to them in a certain way.

That night, she lay in bed feeling relaxed. But as she started dropping off to sleep, she noticed a light coming from her desk. She tried to ignore it. But the light was shining in her eye.

She shuffled over to the desk. It was the Fire and Ice Quartz, glowing.

Elika blinked and ran her thumb over it.

It felt warm.

This was weird. Crystals weren't supposed to glow. Were they?

Elika shrugged. She wrapped the crystal in a sock and buried it in the back corner of her drawer so it wouldn't bug her.

She lay back in bed, ready for sleep.

But the glowing crystal was on her mind.

She wondered what the French word was for 'glow'. She Google Translated it with her smartphone.

"*Lueur*," she said aloud. "What a cool word." She wrote it on her hand.

Then she googled "glowing crystals". Relief filled her when she learned that some crystals did glow. So, it wasn't that weird after all.

She flopped on her back in bed and turned off the light, feeling sleepy. As she drifted off, the word "lueur" was on her mind. She would have to ask Henry how to pronounce it.

Though she fell asleep with a smile on her face, she woke up in the morning with a scowl.

She just had the weirdest dream ever.

Chapter
Three

Elika decided not to mention the glowing Fire and Ice Quartz crystal to her parents. She had done some more searching on Google, and learned that quartz wasn't one of the crystals that glowed.

So it was weird.

Elika preferred to focus on the normal. The crystal sat safely in its sock at the back of her drawer. What was harder to ignore was the awful dream.

All night, she heard a voice.

High and clear, it moaned, "Alone. Alooooone."

But it was just in Elika's mind. When she woke up and listened hard, she couldn't hear anything. So it was just a dream.

The voice was so sad. Elika felt a pain in her heart when it moaned. There was something broken in it. The voice sounded cracked.

"Just like the Fire and Ice crystal," Elika muttered to herself. The crystal had cracks in its interior, though it was smooth to the touch on the outside.

Elika had a lot of time to think about the moaning voice, as she had the same dream every night.

It wasn't a normal voice, for sure. There was something not quite human about it.

"It sounds like a crystal speaking," Elika said to herself one morning. "Or maybe ice."

After two weeks of the dream, Elika finally told her parents about it. But she wasn't too happy about their solution.

As soon as she mentioned the icy sound of the voice, and the glowing crystal, they sent her straight to Aunt Caroline.

Of course they would.

She dealt in weird things after all.

So now Elika stood in front of Aunt Caroline's office door, holding the crystal in its sock. She didn't want to be there. But she had to. No one else would be weird enough to understand the dream.

Elika knocked. Aunt Caroline opened the door right away. She had her work clothes on – jeans, a blouse and a jacket. Her crazy, curly hair was tied up in a ponytail.

Aunt Caroline looked surprised.

"I never expected to see you here," Aunt Caroline said. "Come in, come in." She waved Elika in with a big smile.

The office looked surprisingly normal. There were lots of books on shelves. A big window let in the light. A map of the Himalayan mountains was framed on the wall. Aunt Caroline's computer sat on a light oak desk.

Elika was impressed.

"This is nice," Elika said.

"You look surprised," Aunt Caroline replied.

"Well, I thought there might be, you know, pictures of your best friend," Elika said.

Aunt Caroline gestured to a locked cabinet with a grin.

"Everything about my mountain friend is in there, along with my journals," Aunt Caroline said. "Lots of students and faculty members come in to my office. I can't just tell everybody about him, can I?"

"No, I hope you don't," Elika said. She couldn't

stand the embarrassment of everyone knowing her aunt had that weird side.

"So, why are you here?" Aunt Caroline asked, crossing her arms. "If you don't mind me asking." She looked at Elika with a rare, serious expression and her eyebrows pinched together.

"Um, I have a problem," Elika said.

"Oh," Aunt Caroline said. "And you came to me for help? I'm honored." Her eyebrows relaxed and a smile flit over her face.

Elika sat on a chair. She was silent as she tried to figure out what to mention first, the terribly sad dream or the glowing crystal. Aunt Caroline watched her and chewed her lip in thought.

"Why would you come to me?" Aunt Caroline wondered aloud. "You've never come to me before."

Elika just looked at her, not sure how to begin.

"I know," Aunt Caroline said with a gleeful grin. "It's your dad, isn't it? My little brother used to drive me crazy. I bet he drives you and your mom crazy too."

"No, no," Elika said. "Dad's cool—it's not that. It's this crystal."

Elika took the Fire and Ice Quartz out of the sock. It glowed like a morning star.

"Your crystal?" Aunt Caroline asked. "What's wrong with it?"

"You can't see it glowing?" Elika said, surprised. "My parents couldn't see it, but I thought they were too normal. I thought you'd be able to see it."

"Ah," Caroline said and raised an eyebrow.

"What?" Elika said, hoping she knew something about the crystal.

"You don't think I'm normal?" Caroline said.

"Um. No," Elika said truthfully. "Not really."

"Well," Caroline said. "I'm going to take that as a compliment."

Elika shrugged. If her aunt thought being called not normal was a compliment, it was just another sign she was weird.

"But can you see it glowing?" Elika said. "It's like a star—like in early morning, you know, when the stars are all a little dim."

"Wow," Aunt Caroline said, her eyes wide. "You know, that sounds almost poetic. Do you write poems?"

"No!" Elika said and crossed her arms. "Poetry is weird."

Aunt Caroline sighed deeply.

"Listen. I can't see this glowing," Aunt Caroline said. "But I know this phenomenon. Some things only reveal their power to one person. One special person."

She smiled at Elika, who scowled.

Elika didn't want to be special.

"I don't know why it chose you," Aunt Caroline said, as if reading Elika's thoughts. "But it did."

Chapter
Four

As they sat across from each other in the office, Aunt Caroline asked Elika lots of questions about the crystal and the dream, and wrote notes in her journal. Elika described everything she could possibly think of, including the exact way the moan sounded. She even had to moan 'Aloooone' as high and as sad as the dream voice, while Aunt Caroline recorded it. That made Elika blush with embarrassment.

If that recording ever got out, Elika's attempts to have normal friends would all be ruined. She certainly hoped Henry would never hear it.

Elika was relieved when Aunt Caroline said she was done with questions. It felt like Elika had been in Aunt Caroline's office for hours, but only twenty minutes had passed. She was even more relieved when Aunt Caroline said she'd take the crystal for awhile. Maybe the dreams would stop if it wasn't in her room at night.

"Leave it with me," Aunt Caroline said, reaching for the crystal. "I'll do some tests on it later this afternoon."

Elika gladly handed the crystal over to her aunt. But when Aunt Caroline closed her hand over the crystal, Elika felt a wrench in her heart.

At the same time, Aunt Caroline shouted, "Ow!" and dropped it.

"It burned me," Aunt Caroline said. She had a red mark on her palm.

"It hurt me too," Elika said. She scooped the crystal up and held it to her heart.

"It's not burning you?" Aunt Caroline asked.

Elika shook her head no.

"It's only a little warm," Elika said. "My heart hurt when you took it." She felt soothed now that the crystal was back with her. The quartz glowed gently.

Aunt Caroline got burn cream from a first aid kit she had stashed under the desk, and rubbed it on her palm.

Elika sighed as she put the crystal back in its sock. It looked like she was stuck with it for awhile.

"I hoped if I gave you the crystal, the dream would go away," Elika said, disappointed.

"Yes, I think the crystal and the dream are linked too," Aunt Caroline said, chewing her lip. "But how?"

Aunt Caroline looked off into the distance for awhile. She was silent for a long time.

Elika shifted in her chair.

"Um, Aunt Caroline?" Elika asked.

"Oh, excuse me," Aunt Caroline said. "I realize the crystal has attached itself to you. I was just remembering a time when I had a similar situation. The Amber Giant called to me in a dream too. A book helped me find him. And a doll."

Elika tensed.

"Yes, yes, I know the whole story of the weird way you found the Amber Giant," Elika said. "But I'm sure in this case it's not a giant. Maybe it's just a neighbor or something."

Aunt Caroline studied Elika.

"Does it sound like a human voice to you?" she asked.

Elika thought about how it sounded so high and clear and broken.

"Not really," Elika said. "It sounds like ice speaking, you know, if ice could speak."

Aunt Caroline smiled. "Another bit of poetry from Elika," she said.

Elika frowned.

"Ice speaking," Aunt Caroline said aloud as she wrote it in her journal.

"So it's the voice in the dream and the glowing crystal," Aunt Caroline said. "Anything else you can think of to tell me?"

"That's it," Elika said.

"OK, I'm on it," Aunt Caroline said. "I'll consult my books and try to get some theories going. Meanwhile, if anything changes, if anything new happens, tell me."

Elika nodded. She was relieved to go. But she hesitated at the door.

"Aunt Caroline, do you believe in promises?" Elika asked.

"Of course I do," Aunt Caroline said. "Your grandma used to say a promise is written in the heart. So if you break a promise, you break your own heart."

"Well, could you promise not to tell anyone about my dream, or the weird glowing crystal?" Elika asked. "Except my parents. They already know."

Aunt Caroline thought for a moment, tapping her pen on her notebook.

"I would really like to tell my colleague Edmund," she said. "He might be of help. He's an expert in creatures like giants."

Elika took a deep breath. Already, the fact that she was weird was spreading. First within the family, and now to someone named Edmund.

"OK, but just him," Elika said. "Promise?"

Aunt Caroline put her hands in a prayer position and bowed. It seemed formal enough, and Elika felt she could finally leave the office.

As she walked out of the building and across the grassy lawn of the campus towards Dad's car, she felt lighter. At least someone else knew about Elika's problem, even if it was her crazy aunt. Surely she of all people could figure out what was going on, and what to do about it.

Hopefully, the dream and glowing crystal weirdness would be over soon. And Elika could go back to being the most normal one in her family.

Chapter
Five

It was a hot and sticky afternoon. The summer heat had finally started. Elika licked her vanilla ice cream cone as she walked with her mom to the dry cleaner's. They would spend Saturday shopping and getting errands done for their trip.

But they weren't going to Niagara Falls. That idea had been scrapped.

They were going to Iceland instead.

Elika sighed. She took another lick of ice cream to cheer herself up.

Though she was disappointed, she had to admit there were good reasons for the change in plan.

One, Elika's dreams were getting stronger. She even woke up crying in the night. The voice in her dream was so sad. Instead of just crying out, "Alone," it also moaned, *"Ein. Einmana."*

Her mom said that *ein* meant "alone" in Icelandic. And *einmana* meant "lonely".

Reason two for changing their vacation destination was that Mom had bought the Fire and Ice crystal in Iceland. And reason three, Aunt Caroline found out that in ancient legend, creatures that were linked to a crystal were made of rock or ice. Apparently Iceland had lots of creatures made of strange things like that, like trolls.

So the owner of the sad voice might belong to a monster in Iceland. Which was the last sort of thing Elika wanted to meet. But that's what they were going to Iceland to find.

Elika sighed more deeply and finished her ice cream, crunching on the cone.

Mom picked up a red, frilly blouse and held it up.

"Now, should I get this for your Aunt Nancy?" Mom asked.

Aunt Nancy was Mom's sister. Elika eyed the blouse. It was a little silly-looking to her, but her aunt wore frilly stuff.

"Yeah, I think she'll like it," Elika said.

"And do you like this one?" Mom asked, holding a green sweater up to Elika. "It matches your eyes."

"No need to draw attention to those," Elika said. "Besides, it's summer."

"Nights can get cool in Iceland," Mom said.

"I thought you said it's always day there now," Elika said. "So there are no nights."

"The sun gets low in the sky," Mom said. "It gets cooler."

Elika rolled her green-yellow eyes.

"I don't want anything," she said. "Especially nothing that will remind me of Iceland."

Mom sighed.

"I wish you would be more excited about going," Mom said. "You are half Icelandic."

Elika slumped.

"It's just that we always go there," Elika said. "And last time I was really bored."

"We don't always go!" Mom said. "We haven't been there in three years."

"Well it feels like we were just there," Elika said.

Elika also felt down for another reason. Henry had made fun of her at school when she told him she was going to Iceland instead of Niagara Falls.

He had said, "Iceland? Better bring your ice skates," and laughed. He told a lot of ice jokes. Elika didn't find even one of them funny.

"Cheer up," Mom said. "You know, now that you're older, you and your cousin Susan can go out on your own. To a café or something like that. It will be more fun than last time."

Elika had been Skyping with her cousin Susan since they were young. But they never had that much to say to each other. Still, maybe her cousin could take her out, or maybe she had some cool friends.

Elika shrugged. It might be more fun, if she could go out with Susan.

"OK," Elika said, though she still frowned. "It would be better if I could hang out with people my own age."

"I promise to take you to one cool place too," Mom said and elbowed her.

Elika felt a smile steal its way onto her lips.

"OK," Elika said. "If there is anywhere cool, that is." But she elbowed Mom back to show she was only teasing.

"I'll surprise you," Mom said.

But really, there was only one reason Elika would like Iceland.

"I just want the dreams to stop," Elika said. "So if going to Iceland fixes everything, I will try to enjoy going there."

"That's my girl," Mom said. She held up the green sweater again. "So, can I buy this? It really is your color."

"OK," Elika said, rolling her eyes. "Maybe we can use it somewhere else too—like if we go to Niagara Falls this winter."

Her mom chewed her lip and looked at Elika with a serious expression.

"What?" Elika asked.

"When your Aunt Caroline met the Amber Giant, it led her down a path that changed her life," her mom said. "Look at her now- a geology professor, going to Nepal every chance she can get. She's in the Himalayas months at a time."

"So?" Elika said.

"Well, I wonder, when you meet the owner of

the voice, and the crystal, what will happen to you?"
Mom said.

Elika thought for a moment.

"I don't think anything will happen to me," Elika
said. "I'll give the Thing, whatever it is, the crystal,
and then come home and be normal."

"Are you sure about that?" Mom asked.

"Well, if you think I will want to go to Iceland for
months at a time, you're wrong," Elika said.

A smile played on Mom's lips.

"I could think of worse things," Mom said.

They bought the frilly blouse and green sweater.
They also picked up a purse for Elika's cousin. As
they walked to the car in the summer heat, Elika
pondered something that gave her the chills.

"Mom?" Elika asked.

"Hmmm?" Mom said, getting out her car keys.

"Do you really think the voice could belong to
something like a giant?" Elika asked.

Her mom shrugged.

"Maybe. Hopefully something smaller," Mom
said. "Though maybe hearing giants runs in the
family."

Elika's shoulders slumped.

She might be just as weird as Aunt Caroline.

She couldn't think of anything worse.

Chapter
Six

The trip to Iceland had just gotten worse.

Aunt Caroline met them at the airport.

"Aunt Caroline is coming?" Elika exclaimed when she saw her aunt come up to them at check-in with a backpack.

"Of course," her mom said. "She's our expert in glowing crystals and creatures who speak in dreams." Her mom elbowed Elika.

"Shh!" Elika said, looking around nervously. She hoped no one heard that strange sentence.

"She's not staying with us, is she?" Elika asked. Dad shushed her as Aunt Caroline came near.

"Try to be nice," her mom said under her breath. "She's helping you out."

But Aunt Caroline didn't seem to be coming just to help Elika out. She seemed genuinely excited to go, and talked constantly when they got on the plane. For some reason, she sat right next to Elika.

"As a geologist, I can't wait to get there," Aunt Caroline said once they took off. "The rock formations, the glaciers. It's one of the most active volcanic regions on the Earth. The geysers!"

Aunt Caroline clapped her hands.

"As someone who is interested in giants and other creatures," Aunt Caroline said, lowering her voice. "Iceland is the perfect place to go. And I've never been anywhere but Nepal!"

"Really?" Elika asked, surprised. "I thought with your job—you know, you'd go all sorts of weird places."

Aunt Caroline shook her head.

"I do get away to conferences on the East Coast, here in the US," Aunt Caroline said. "But the Amber Giant gets lonely without me. So I need to spend a lot of time in Nepal."

Elika hadn't realized the giant got lonely.

"I thought you wanted to be in the Himalayas all the time," Elika said. "So, you just go to keep him company?"

"You read the story I wrote for Sammy so you know. I'm his Master," Aunt Caroline said. "Though I never order him around or misuse that power, there is still a bond. He misses me."

"Do you miss him?" Elika asked.

"Of course," Aunt Caroline said. "But I could see him once a year and be happy with that. I would love to travel other places. But he's...well, clingy. The Sherpas say he cries a lot when I'm not there. Especially at night."

Elika had never thought a giant could be clingy. That explained why Aunt Caroline went to the mountains so much. She actually felt a little bad for the giant.

"You should come sometime," Aunt Caroline said. "Kathmandu is a fascinating city."

Elika sank into her chair and said something noncommittal. She was definitely not interested in meeting a giant.

Elika took out her book on crystals and pretended to read. Luckily, her aunt had a few books too and didn't try to talk to her for the rest of the flight.

Her mom's sister picked them up at the airport

and shuttled them to her place. The house looked familiar, and memories of being there three years ago came back to her as they walked through the front door into the small living room.

Last time, Elika had a room to herself. This time, they gave the guest room to Aunt Caroline. Elika was a little worried she'd have to share with Aunt Caroline, but she was given a place to sleep in her cousin's bedroom.

Elika hung out on the air bed in the bedroom for a few boring hours until her cousin Susan walked in.

Elika felt a rush of happiness to see her. They hugged, and she gave Susan the purse, which she liked.

Elika's cousin looked much more Chinese than Elika did. She had straight black hair like Elika, but normal, dark brown eyes and normal cheeks, rather than Elika's green eyes and high cheekbones.

"You look great," Elika said, and meant it.

"You too," Susan said. "What are you doing?"

"Listening to a French Mp3," Elika said. "I'm learning French."

"Me too!" Susan said. "At school."

"I'm doing an online course," Elika said. "And a guy at school from France teaches me some words."

"You know a real French guy?" Susan said. "That is so cool."

They traded French words until dinner. It was kind of fun.

But after dinner, things got boring again. Elika lay in the dark on the bed, not feeling remotely sleepy. Not only did she not want to have the dream again, she was aware that outside, through the thick, blackout curtains, it was daylight. Somehow she knew, and it was too weird for sleep.

It took hours of listening to French Mp3s, but Elika finally fell asleep.

When she woke up, Susan was staring at her. The light was on.

"Did you have a nightmare or something?" Susan said.

"No," Elika lied. In fact, she had been dreaming about the sad, moaning voice.

"You were moaning," Susan said.

"I was moaning?" Elika said. "That's weird."

"It was weird," Susan said.

"I'll try to be more quiet," Elika said.

"Please do." Susan flipped off the light and sank back into her bed.

Elika lay awake. Her cheeks burned with embarrassment. She didn't want to fall asleep and start moaning again.

She stayed awake until morning, vowing not to sleep again until they found whatever it was that was sending her the dream.

She wrote 'do not sleep' on her hand.

It ended up being one of the harder promises to keep.

Chapter
Seven

The next morning at 5 a.m., Elika went downstairs to the breakfast table. She was the first one up. Elika sighed. Still, sunlight shone strongly through the window, so it was morning enough for breakfast.

She had a spoonful of cereal halfway to her mouth and was staring into space thinking about how much she wanted to go to sleep, when Aunt Caroline walked in.

"Did you get any sleep, Elika?" Aunt Caroline asked.

Elika shook her head no, feeling groggy with tiredness.

Aunt Caroline said that if Elika couldn't sleep, they better solve the mystery of the dream sooner rather than later.

It was almost a relief when Aunt Caroline took

Elika in the rental car towards the southeast part of Iceland. Almost a relief, because after all she was with Aunt Caroline.

Elika didn't want to spend so much time alone with her weird aunt. At least she did not have to hide the dream from her. In fact, her aunt said if Elika moaned in her sleep, it was OK, she would understand. So Elika could even nap in the car.

She changed the promise on her hand from 'do not sleep' to 'do not sleep at cousin Susan's house'.

Elika watched out the car window as they passed the little shops and cafes of Reykjavik. The sun was high and strong, and it looked like afternoon rather than morning.

They drove in silence for awhile, as the city receded and they were surrounded by countryside. Aunt Caroline pointed out an old lava flow, hardened into rock over the centuries. Tiny flowers grew on it.

Elika dropped off to sleep, exhausted.

The dream started immediately.

"*Ein*," a voice entered her mind. "*Einmana. Aloooooone.*"

Something was different this time. Elika could

see ice everywhere. Sunlight shone through walls of ice as if she were in a cave.

Elika woke with a start.

"Did you have the dream?" Aunt Caroline asked, her voice excited.

"Yeah," Elika said, rubbing her eyes. "This time I saw something too. I think she's in an ice cave or something. Are there ice caves?"

Aunt Caroline nodded yes.

"That's where we're going. In fact I thought the best bet was Vatnajökull glacier," Caroline said. "It's very old, and full of ice caves. Have you been there?"

"I've never been to the glacier," Elika said. "We just stay in Reykjavik when we come visit. Oh, on one visit we went to see weird birds—puffins."

"Well, my colleague Edmund, who I mentioned to you before, lives in Hofn, just at the edge of the glacier," Aunt Caroline said. "Edmund is on a business trip unfortunately, but I've been emailing him about your dream. Get this, he says in Hofn there have recently been reports of a high voice on the wind."

"Do you think it could be the same voice from my dream?" Elika asked.

"Could be," Aunt Caroline said. "Edmund has given me some ideas of which parts of the glacier to investigate. The ice caves have quite a lot of mythology surrounding them—old stories of giants and trolls."

"Great," Elika said, and rolled her eyes. "What are the chances she's like, a tiny fairy rather than a giant?"

Aunt Caroline shrugged.

"I'm going on what I've learned and read," Aunt Caroline said. "But I'm also going on instinct. My hypothesis is that we're looking for an ice-based creature. Fairies aren't made of ice, as far as I know."

They sat in silence awhile longer. Elika didn't really want to think about fairies, ice-based or otherwise. She tried to think of something else.

They passed mountains and fields. She noticed something painted on the bigger rocks in the fields.

"Aunt Caroline?" Elika asked. "What are those little painted doors on the rocks for?"

"Elves," Aunt Caroline said. "They are elf houses.

The farmers don't want to disturb them, so they mark the stones with doors."

Elika bit her lip.

She really wished she hadn't asked.

The road came down by the coast. The sapphire-blue water under the bright sun greeted Elika's eyes. She gazed at the ocean's beauty.

"I have a question for you," Aunt Caroline said, breaking the silence.

"Go ahead," Elika said.

"Why do you think the voice in your dream belongs to a 'she'?" Aunt Caroline asked.

"Oh," Elika said. "I guess it sounds like a woman."

"A female," Aunt Caroline said. "Interesting. Giants and trolls tend to be males."

Elika thought about that for awhile.

"How do they, you know, make baby giants and trolls then?" Elika asked.

Aunt Caroline pinched her.

"That, my friend, is one of the big questions we scientists like to ask," Aunt Caroline said. "We just don't know. Maybe that's why there are so few of those creatures in the world. Anyway, if your creature is female, she could be quite rare."

"Aren't giants and trolls rare anyway?" Elika asked.

"Good point," Caroline said. "I guess the Amber Giant has been in my life so long, I forget."

Elika hoped she would never reach a point in her life that she thought giants were normal.

Her stomach rumbled. It was so bright outside it could be lunchtime, but then again it was bright when they left. It could still be morning.

She checked her phone. 1 p.m. So, definitely lunchtime.

Aunt Caroline had packed cheese sandwiches, and Elika brought them out. They ate as her aunt drove along the road. It was a smooth road, and Elika caught glimpses of the ocean. The road went along the south coast.

Her belly was full and the drive soothed her. Elika fell into a rare, dreamless sleep.

When she woke, she felt refreshed. The car was stopped in front of a hotel. Though it still seemed like afternoon based on the sun, Aunt Caroline said they had made it all the way to Hofn.

Elika got out of the car. It felt so good to stretch her legs. She was relaxed and sleepy after her nap. Though that didn't last long. A blast of chilly wind blew through, waking her up.

It was much colder here than in Reykjavik. She wished she had a coat over her new, green sweater.

Aunt Caroline said they would eat dinner, go to sleep, then hike into the glacier in the morning. She glanced nervously at the icy mountain in front of her. Though Aunt Caroline loved freezing mountains, Elika would rather be in warmer places. Elika hoped she could keep up with her. She had seen so many photos of Aunt Caroline in jeans and crampons, holding things like climbing ropes and ice axes. Elika had never climbed a mountain before. She wasn't even that fond of walking up hills in her neighborhood.

She shivered. At least the glacier would wait until the morning. For now, she could look forward to a hot dinner and a comfortable bed.

She was definitely not looking forward to the morning.

Chapter Eight

The hotel turned out to be really nice. After a dinner of delicious pasta, Elika and Aunt Caroline retired to their rooms. Whoever Edmund was must be a nice guy. He had managed to book them two rooms under a discounted rate. Puffy ski jackets and crampons in their sizes were waiting on their beds. Elika was especially happy about the warm ski jacket. Aunt Caroline was also given a camping stove and instant meals, which she stuffed into her backpack.

Elika took a long, hot shower. She sprawled out on the white comforter and was quickly asleep.

The dream started again. Ice walls reflected light. This time, though, the ice cave wasn't turquoise. It was pink, orange and red. Elika wondered why.

The moan began, loud and clear.

"Alooone," the voice moaned. "*Eeeeeiiiin.*"

Elika woke up. The wind howled outside. And a very faint, high sound just like the voice in the dream seemed to say, "*Eeeiiiin.*"

Could she hear the voice outside her dream now?

Elika sprang out of bed and ran to Aunt Caroline's door. She had to knock several times before Aunt Caroline finally answered. Her dark, curly hair was a mess, and her eyes squinted at Elika.

"What is it?" Aunt Caroline asked, rubbing her tired eyes. "Are you OK?"

"The voice!" Elika said. "I think I can hear it, outside my dream—like, for real." Elika poked her head in Aunt Caroline's room. She couldn't hear much, except for a mechanical hum like a generator.

"It's stronger in my room, come listen," Elika said. She took Aunt Caroline's hand and led her across the hallway.

They stood silently in Elika's room, listening to the wind. A voice seemed to climb over the wind, moaning.

"Hear it?" Elika whispered.

"I can hear something," Aunt Caroline said. "It could just be the wind. But yes, I could also imagine it was saying 'ein'. Does it sound like the voice in your dream?"

Elika nodded.

"It's the same, except a lot fainter," she said.

Aunt Caroline's eyes grew wider.

"Listen, I'll make a cup of coffee and then we can drive into the mountain and follow the voice," Aunt Caroline said.

"In the dark?" Elika asked. The clock by her bedside read 3 a.m.

Aunt Caroline grinned at her.

"It's not dark," her aunt said. She opened Elika's blackout curtains.

Elika gasped. The sky was streaked with pink, orange and red. She had never seen a sky like that.

"Sunrise," Caroline said. She fiddled with the coffee maker in Elika's room.

"Maybe that's why the cave in my dream was pink and orange," Elika said. "Would the sunrise color the ice?"

"Your dream may be in real-time," Caroline said,

nodding yes. She made a steaming hot cup of coffee for herself, and handed Elika a hot chocolate.

"Drink up," Caroline said. "It's cold on the glacier."

Elika shuddered in anticipation. She curled her hands around the hot mug, hoping this wasn't the last warm drink she would have for awhile.

Once they finished their drinks and packed what they needed for the glacier, Elika followed Aunt Caroline to the car. In the chilly air, Elika pulled the collar of her ski jacket as high as it would go.

The wind picked up. It blew Elika's hair around her face. She pulled it into a ponytail and wished she had a hat, as the cold air chilled her neck.

They drove with the windows down so they could follow the voice. It made it super-cold in the car. Even though she wore the ski jacket over her sweater, Elika had to wrap a blanket around herself.

Aunt Caroline didn't seem to be bothered by the cold. In fact, she looked happy.

"I think I hear it more clearly now," Aunt Caroline said with excitement in her voice. They had been driving for an hour up a dirt road that skirted the glacier. Elika had expected ice and snow, but they were still low enough that bare rock covered the landscape. Aunt Caroline explained that no roads actually went into the glacier from here. So, at some point soon they would have to get out and walk.

Elika suddenly felt something hot by her foot.

"Um, Aunt Caroline?" Elika said.

"Mm?" Aunt Caroline said, craning her neck out the window as she drove.

"The crystal in my backpack is weirdly hot," Elika said. It was too hot to touch even through the sock it was in. She managed to hold one end of the sock and pull it out of her pack.

"Ouch!" Elika said when the hot crystal sock touched her palm. She put the sock on the dashboard.

"It's hot?" Caroline said with a gleam of excitement in her eyes. "It could be another sign we're getting close to the creature."

The road bent back towards the coast, so they had to stop. Ice and snow coated the rocks around them. They could drive no farther into the glacier.

The voice still moaned. Somewhere in the vast

expanse of ice was a lonely creature.

They stepped onto the icy dirt, and Elika braced herself for freezing wind. But the wind had calmed down.

Snow was piled up on rocks and in mounds everywhere. The sky was cloudy, and the sun was hidden.

As they listened, Elika felt it was almost too quiet. Even the moan stopped.

"I don't hear anything," Elika said.

"Keep listening," Aunt Caroline said. "I bet it starts up again."

Elika shivered. She had the feeling that she was being watched. She shrugged it off. It was probably just the cold air creeping down her neck.

"Fire!" Aunt Caroline suddenly shouted.

With a shock, Elika saw that smoke filled the car.

Aunt Caroline opened the door and threw water from her water bottle on the flames. She took a stick, pulled something small and flaming out of the car and threw it in the snow. Steam rose from it.

"The crystal?" Elika said, surprised.

"It melted a hole in the dashboard," Aunt

Caroline said. "How amazing!"

Elika didn't think it was amazing. It was downright weird and a little scary.

The crystal sat in a puddle by the car. It melted the ice around it. Elika hovered her hand over the crystal. It gave off heat like a burning piece of coal.

"How will we carry it now?" Elika asked.

"We may not have to," Aunt Caroline said. Her gaze was fixed on something in the distance. Elika looked out, but didn't see anything.

But after a few breaths, she saw it. A great, big shape that walked across a flat expanse of sheer ice. It moved like a walking boulder.

Elika gasped. She ran into the car and shut the door.

She hoped it would go away.

But the enormous figure was coming closer.

Chapter
Nine

Elika stared at the huge figure walking across the icy landscape towards them from the car. Her heart beat fast with fear. Aunt Caroline was still outside, and Elika was afraid for them both.

She rolled the car window down.

"Aunt Caroline!" Elika yelled. "Get in the car! Let's leave the crystal and go."

But Aunt Caroline actually walked towards the huge, moving shape. Elika felt the whole car shaking as it came closer.

It was as big as a T-Rex, and shaped sort of like a human, except it looked like it was made of ice.

An ice giant.

Elika was too scared to breathe.

The giant walked right by Aunt Caroline, throwing a shadow as big as a giant redwood tree with its ice-blue body. It went straight to the crystal. Its massive knees bent as it crouched down to look at it.

When it turned to Elika, she was struck by the intelligence in the creature's large, light blue eyes.

"Gift?" it asked. "You bring me this gift?" Its voice was high and clear, just like the moaning voice in Elika's dreams. The giant held the crystal up to examine it. It didn't seem to be melting its icy hand.

Elika nodded slowly. She wished the window was rolled up, but she was too scared to move.

"Gift," Elika said. "For you." Her voice came out very quiet, as she was afraid.

"Come out," the giant said. "Let me see you."

Elika shook her head no. She wished Aunt Caroline would jump in the car and drive them away.

"We have to go," Elika said. "Aunt Caroline!" she yelled.

Her aunt came up right next to the giant. Now Elika was more afraid for her aunt than herself. The giant looked like it could crush her with one ice fist.

"Have you been calling 'Alone' and 'Ein'?" Aunt

Caroline said in a normal voice, as if she was making chit-chat. "My niece Elika hears this in her dreams."

The giant's blue eyes grew wider and it stared at Elika.

"I did not know a human heard me," the giant said. "I have been calling for years. Longer than most humans live."

The Ice Giant scowled. Its eyes looked fierce.

"I don't like humans," it said. "I would not have called if I knew it would bring humans."

The Ice Giant clenched its huge, ice fist.

"I was calling giants," she said. Its square jaw clenched.

Now even Aunt Caroline looked worried. Her eyebrows knit together.

"Elika, do you feel you can let go of the crystal now?" Aunt Caroline said. "Do you feel the pain in your heart that you felt when you gave it to me?"

Elika shook her head no.

"I'm fine," Elika said.

"OK, let's go," Aunt Caroline said.

Finally, Aunt Caroline was on the same page as Elika. Hopefully they could drive away without the giant getting angrier.

But the giant surprised them. "Go?" the Ice Giant said. "But you just got here. Stay."

"I thought you just said you don't like humans," Elika said. "We can leave, no problem."

"But you brought me a rare gift," the Ice Giant said. "I must welcome you in my cave in return."

Aunt Caroline's eyes gleamed.

"A chance to see where it lives!" Aunt Caroline mumbled to herself, loud enough for Elika to hear.

"Aunt Caroline!" Elika said. "She said she doesn't like humans. Wait—" She turned to the Ice Giant. "Are you a she?" she asked.

"Of course!" the Ice Giant said, her eyes wide and astonished.

"Um, well, it's cold, and there's no phone signal, so we really should go," Elika said apologetically. "My parents will worry."

Aunt Caroline sighed. "I guess you're right," she said. "Let's go."

Before Aunt Caroline could get back in the car, the creature pinched the back tire with her finger and thumb until it popped.

"There," the Ice Giant said. "I have seen many of these human-movers. They will not work when that wheel is flat."

"Um..." Aunt Caroline eyed the tire. "Come on, Elika. Let's stay for a little while. What an opportunity!"

Elika got shakily out of the car. She stood close to Aunt Caroline.

"Don't worry," Aunt Caroline whispered to her as they followed the Ice Giant, who beckoned to them. "I have a spare tire."

"I don't have a good feeling about this," Elika said. Her knees wobbled with fear.

"We'll be fine," Aunt Caroline said. "I just know it. Now, let's see her ice cave. This is so fascinating!"

Elika sneaked a peek at her phone. Still no signal.

She gulped. No one knew exactly where they were. She had last texted her mom from Hofn.

Elika dragged her feet. It was cold, the crampons in her bag dug into her back, and they were following an Ice Giant deeper into the mountains.

She had a strong feeling they should turn around and run, drive the car even with the flat tire and get back to Hofn. But the giant kept close to them, and kept turning around to usher them along.

For now, it seemed they were stuck.

Chapter
Ten

The enormous Ice Giant led Aunt Caroline and Elika deeper into the glacier. Elika's heart beat rapidly with fear and she had a strong desire to hold Aunt Caroline's hand. She felt too old for that, though. So she didn't.

After about an hour of walking, Elika's fear was replaced by exhaustion. Her thighs burned and her legs were heavy. She fell on the ice twice, and was wet from landing in the snow.

It was a relief when they reached the vast opening of an ice cave. Elika held her sides and gasped for breath. She tried to sit on a rock and slipped, ending up knocking her elbow on the icy ground, which would leave a painful bruise.

The Ice Giant entered the cave, and beckoned them to follow.

Aunt Caroline, who hadn't slipped once and was not gasping at all, patted Elika's back where she sat.

"Are you OK, kiddo?" Aunt Caroline asked.

Elika nodded, still breathing heavily.

"I'm just not made for mountains," she said between gasps. "At least I'm still alive and kicking, as grandma used to say."

"That's the spirit," Aunt Caroline said.

"Do you think we should run?" Elika asked. The Ice Giant wasn't watching them. She had disappeared into the cave.

Aunt Caroline shook her head no.

"There's no way we could outrun her," she said quietly to Elika. "Her legs are so long, like two tree trunks."

Elika turned her face up to the sun, which had broken through the clouds, high in the sky. It warmed her cheeks. It felt good to sit still.

Her quiet moment didn't last long. The Ice Giant poked her massive head out of the cave, startling them both. Elika felt fear coming back, turning her stomach.

"Come in, come in," she said to Elika.

Aunt Caroline took her hand. Elika was glad she did. It made her feel braver. They followed the giant into the cave together.

The walls and floor of the cave were mostly ice, with dark rock here and there. Sunlight shone through the ice, filling it with turquoise light. Elika's eyes grew wide with amazement.

"It's like being in one of my crystals," Elika said to Aunt Caroline. Her aunt squeezed her hand in response.

Lots of snow was piled in the corners of the cave. Elika wondered if it actually snowed inside. It certainly looked like it.

They stopped by a flow of ice that looked like a river frozen in time. The ice had a green streak in it, a similar color to her own eyes. It was cold and solid to the touch.

Aunt Caroline laced on her crampons. Elika pulled hers out of her backpack and did the same, as the Ice Giant watched them.

"I love crampons," Aunt Caroline said, walking easily. "They are so useful."

"I have seen humans wear those before," the

giant said in her high, clear voice.

"It's the first time for me, though I have worn ice skates before," Elika said. She took a few tentative steps. Her legs felt strange and wobbly.

"Ice skates?" the Ice Giant asked. "What are those?"

"There are blades on the shoes," Elika explained. "So you can glide over the ice."

"Ah," the giant said. "I have seen humans wear those on lakes in the winter."

"A boy at my school told me I'd have to wear ice skates in Iceland, because the whole place was covered with ice," Elika said, and laughed at the memory. "I told him he was wrong, but now I guess he was right." She hoped she'd see Henry again, even if it was just to tell him how icy it was.

The Ice Giant only stared at her in response. It was unnerving and Elika gulped.

The giant led them through an archway, which narrowed into a tunnel. The walls, ceiling and floor were all ice.

They crunched across the ice floor deep into the cave. It was colder in the tunnel, and darker.

Elika blinked when they exited the tunnel into a bigger chamber—a huge room made of ice with a vaulted ceiling. It had smooth, reflective walls and the high ceiling was carved with stars and the moon. Elika gasped, and Aunt Caroline echoed her thoughts.

"Beautiful," Aunt Caroline said.

"This is my home," the Ice Giant said to Elika. "You are the first humans to enter it."

Elika looked around. There wasn't anything but ice, rock and piles of snow.

Aunt Caroline seemed to be thinking what Elika was thinking.

"Where are your things?" Aunt Caroline said. "It's awfully empty in here. Don't you have possessions?"

"No," the Ice Giant said. She clenched her fist, and looked angrily at Aunt Caroline. Elika shivered. But Aunt Caroline didn't seem frightened.

"Where do you sit?" Elika asked, thinking that she would like to sit down somewhere herself. The crampons made her feel unbalanced.

"Sit?" the giant said, her eyes hard.

"I mean, do you have a great big chair?" Elika

asked, her voice shaking with nerves.

The giant looked at Elika and her jaw softened. She replied in a quieter voice.

"I don't need a chair," the giant said. "I don't need much."

She opened her hand to show them Elika's crystal.

"I have the gift," she said. "That is enough."

The giant looked closely at Elika.

"You are a little small for a human," she said. "How old are you?"

"I'm thirteen," Elika said. Her voice came out weak. She was afraid. She cleared her throat and spoke up more bravely. "Thirteen," she said more loudly.

"Thirteen!" the Ice Giant said. "So young. But you seem older."

Elika shrugged.

"Just as well," the Ice Giant said. "If you had a husband or a betrothed, he would have to move here with you."

"M-m-move here?" Elika said, shocked.

"Yes," the Ice Giant said. "Welcome to my home,

which is your home now." The giant smiled, and her ice teeth shined in brilliant light.

Elika felt horrified. Aunt Caroline squeezed her hand.

How were they going to get out of the cave?

Chapter
Eleven

Elika tried to argue with the giant. There was just no way she was going to live in an ice cave.

"Why do you want me to live here?" Elika said. "You don't even like humans."

"I think that I like you," the Ice Giant said. "Which is strange because I truly do not like humans. I need to know more about you. Where did you live, before you came to live with me?"

A prickle climbed up Elika's neck at the giant's words. Did the giant really think she was going to live here in the cave? Elika certainly planned to leave as soon as she could.

Aunt Caroline grabbed her hand again and squeezed, as if giving Elika confidence.

"Where I live now," Elika said, stressing the present tense, "is New York. It's far away, across the ocean."

"She's just a child, really." Aunt Caroline jumped in. "She is not as strong as an adult human. She'll freeze if we stay here longer."

"Hmm," the Ice Giant said. "I will give her my sun garment. That will help." The giant strode out of the enormous room in just a few steps.

"Sun garment!" Aunt Caroline said. "I wonder what that looks like."

"Aunt Caroline!" Elika said, feeling panicked. "I can't live here with her!"

Aunt Caroline chewed her lip.

"I have a plan," she said. "I am going to—"

The return of the Ice Giant interrupted her. Elika's heart sank. She wanted to hear Aunt Caroline's plan.

The giant held an enormous garment made of leaves twined together.

"Wrap this around yourself," the giant said, offering it to Elika. "You will be warmer."

Elika couldn't lift it. It was too massive. It fell to the ground, and she pulled a corner of the leaf garment around herself. She was instantly warmer.

"It helps, but I'm still kind of cold," Elika shivered. "I'd like to go back in the sun now."

"I have an idea," Aunt Caroline said to the giant. "We have a camping stove in the trunk of the car. It will help Elika stay warm. It's controlled fire."

The Ice Giant's eyes grew big and fierce. She clenched her fist at Aunt Caroline.

"Fire is not a friend," she said angrily.

"No, this wouldn't be a threat to you or your cave," Aunt Caroline said. "It's only a very small contraption. I have some food we can heat up too, and Elika will be warm that way."

"Hmmm," the Ice Giant said. She looked at Elika, who shivered visibly.

"I suppose you don't eat ice, like me?" the Ice Giant asked.

Elika shook her head no.

"Very well, then," the Ice Giant said. "I will go get it."

"Do you know what it looks like?" Aunt Caroline said. "Do you know how to open the car?"

"You will tell me," the giant said.

Aunt Caroline shook her head no.

"It's best I go," Aunt Caroline said. "If you handle the camping stove the wrong way, it will explode."

Elika realized that was a lie, but she kept quiet.

"We will all go, then," the Ice Giant said. "You can handle this Camp-Ing Stove. Though I will need to wear the sun garment, as the sun is high and hot."

"Elika's not going to make it there and back," Aunt Caroline said. "She is exhausted."

Elika faked sleepy eyes, and curled up in the leaf garment. She didn't know what Aunt Caroline's plan was, but it seemed wise to play along with it. Also, she really was too exhausted to walk all the way back to the car and the cave again.

"I'll go on my own," Aunt Caroline said. "I know the way, I'm fast, and I can bring the stove, food, and a few blankets back here."

The Ice Giant studied Aunt Caroline closely.

"OK," the Ice Giant said. "I lose nothing. If you don't come back, I don't care. Elika is the one I want to stay."

A sinking feeling hit Elika in the gut. Was Aunt Caroline's plan to run away and leave her alone?

As if noticing her fear, Aunt Caroline grabbed Elika and held her close.

"I will come back," she whispered into Elika's ear.

"I promise. And a promise is written in the heart."

Then she left the cave, her crampons crunching away.

Elika hid her face in the leaf garment as tears slipped from her eyes.

The thought of Aunt Caroline not coming back was too awful to bear.

She had never felt so alone.

Chapter
Twelve

Elika cried herself to sleep in the leaf garment when Aunt Caroline left. A few hours later, she woke up feeling calmer. She was warm in the ski jacket and leaf cloak.

The cave was beautiful. The turquoise walls were lined with light blue and white.

There was even half a chocolate bar in the pocket of the jacket. She sent a silent thanks to Aunt Caroline's colleague Edmund as she devoured it.

It was quiet and still in the cave. The Ice Giant was sitting cross-legged with her eyes closed in the corner. She seemed to be meditating. Could Elika leave the cave without her knowing?

Elika shifted to stand up. The Ice Giant immediately opened her light blue eyes.

Elika pretended to stretch. She didn't want the

giant to know she was trying to escape.

When the giant met Elika's gaze, she smiled. After the cold scowls on her face before, Elika was surprised to see a friendly expression.

"It's OK to cry," the giant said to Elika. "I cry too."

"I'm OK now," Elika said, a little embarrassed that the giant had witnessed her sobs.

The giant crawled towards Elika, and her movements were fluid and relaxed. More like water than ice.

"Now that she is gone, I must thank you for the gift," she said, holding the crystal. "As I hold it, my heart feels better. Happier."

"You really just have this crystal and the sun garment?" Elika asked. She wondered if no one had ever given the giant a gift before.

The giant shook her head no. She went to a corner of the cave and moved a boulder aside. She pulled out a big, beautiful conch shell, which was white and peach-colored.

"My husband gave me this," she said. "On our wedding."

Elika imagined her husband was another Ice

Giant. Possibly even bigger than this giant. She looked around nervously.

"Your husband?" Elika said. "Where is he?"

"Fifty years ago he fell off a cliff," the giant said. "He shattered." She frowned.

"Oh," Elika said. "I'm so sorry."

A great tear formed and froze into a snowflake. More snowflakes fell from the giant's eyes. Elika wanted to make a snowball out of them. But she reminded herself the Ice Giant was crying. They were sad snowflakes.

Elika realized all the snow mounds in the cave must be from the Ice Giant's tears. She was surprised the giant was so sad after fifty years of being without her husband. She must have loved him a lot. Elika remembered how the giant had moaned 'lonely' in her dream. This was one sad giant.

"Don't you have any friends?" Elika said in a soft voice. "Other giants?"

The Ice Giant shook her head.

"My husband and I were the last Ice People in this area," the Ice Giant said. "The others moved up north a century ago. Too many humans here, too much disruption."

"Why don't you go up north to find them?" Elika asked.

"Alone?" the Ice Giant said, and shook her head. "I don't want to make the journey alone. Too dangerous."

"Dangerous?" Elika asked. "What could you possibly be afraid of?"

The Ice Giant stared at her.

"Oh well, I guess cliffs," Elika said, remembering that her husband had fallen and shattered.

"Melting, too," the giant said. "The journey can only be done in the winter, when the sun hides. Even then, geysers erupt and cover everything with very hot water. Too dangerous for Ice People, unless they know the way."

"Are you actually made of ice?" Elika asked. "Like, can hot water melt you?"

The giant reached out her hand. Elika felt it.

"So smooth, so cold," Elika said. "It does feel like ice."

"What are you made of?" the giant asked. "Your hand feels hot and soft."

Elika had to think about it. She knew she wasn't made of ice, but she wasn't sure what she was made of, exactly.

"Lots of things," Elika said. "Well, I couldn't melt, or shatter, I don't think."

The Ice Giant studied the conch shell in her hands. Her eyes were sad. A few more snowflakes fell from them.

For the first time, Elika felt sad for the giant rather than afraid. She couldn't imagine being all alone for fifty years.

No wonder the Ice Giant had moaned "alone" through the long and empty nights.

Chapter
Thirteen

The Ice Giant was staring sadly at the shell in her hands. Elika wondered how she could cheer the giant up.

"Did you make the moon-and-stars ceiling?" Elika said. The ceiling of the cave was covered in constellations.

"No," the giant said. "My ancestors made that." She put the conch shell down and sniffed heavily. Then she came nearer to Elika.

"So," the giant said and smiled. "Enough about me. What about you?"

"What about me?" Elika said.

"Are you an Other?" the giant asked.

Elika had no idea what the Ice Giant meant, and said so.

"Your eyes," the giant said. "I have met humans

with brown eyes, blue eyes, and yes, sometimes green, though not yellow-green like yours. Some humans even have such light, clear blue eyes like us ice people. But your eyes...I have never seen eyes like that. So I think you might have Other blood. Was one of your ancestors Other?"

Elika didn't know what to say. She didn't know what Others were, but she didn't like the sound of them. They sounded weird.

"I'm just human," Elika said. "All my ancestors are human."

"Hmm," the giant said as if she didn't believe Elika. "You could also hear me in your dream."

"Well," Elika said. "Aunt Caroline heard her giant in her dream too."

"You know another giant?" the Ice Giant said. "Ice, like me?"

"He's not ice," Elika said. "Though he lives in the cold, high in the mountains, in the snow."

"I want to meet him!" the Ice Giant said. "I have not seen another giant in a long time."

"Oh, he's far away though," Elika said. "The Himalayas."

The Ice Giant looked off into the distance with a faraway expression.

"Yes, I have heard of those mountains," she said. "Old, old places, and giants lived there long ago. Though we do not use the term 'giants'. We call them 'People of the Yak'. It is in our story."

"Your story?" Elika asked, wondering what she meant.

"Come with me," the giant said. She crawled into a low tunnel of ice that lead out of the large chamber.

Curious, Elika followed. They entered another big room, and she gasped.

There was an enormous wall of ice in front of her. It was covered with writing that looked like hieroglyphics. The symbols were deep in the ice.

"Is this chiseled in?" Elika asked. She felt the wall, but it was smooth. She couldn't feel any impressions or chisel marks.

"No. It's the old way of ice writing," the Ice Giant said. "We Ice People don't know how our ancestors wrote it. We can only read it in the light. Never in the winter. It's deep in the wall."

"Wow," Elika said. She took her phone out of her pocket and snapped a picture.

"See, my husband's name is also in ice writing," the Ice Giant said and showed Elika her leg. A series of symbols were visible deep in the giant's leg.

"We Ice People use ice writing when we make a promise," the giant explained. "Like when I married my husband. But we do not know how to use ice writing outside our own bodies, like on this wall before us. That has been lost to the Ice People."

"Wow," Elika said. She placed her forehead on the smooth ice wall, and watched sunlight play on the symbols within it.

"It's our story," the Ice Giant said. "The story of the Ice People. We also sing it to remember."

"Aunt Caroline would love this," Elika said. Her forehead was numb with cold from pressing it to the ice.

The Ice Giant scowled.

"I will not show it to her," she said.

"Oh, I didn't like her either at first," Elika said. "But Aunt Caroline's OK, once you get to know her."

The Ice Giant clenched her fist.

"I don't like humans," she said. "Except for you." She gave Elika a brilliant smile that reflected the light.

"Oh," Elika said. "Thanks. I think."

"We'll be best friends," the Ice Giant said. "You can live in another, small part of the cave. I will show you. It is more rock than ice. It will be warmer."

Elika shuddered. Nervousness and cold returned to her and chilled her. She just had to find a way to escape the cave. She didn't know what Aunt Caroline's plan was, but she couldn't rely on it.

Hours had passed, and there was no sign of her aunt.

Elika liked to think Aunt Caroline was coming back. She had promised, after all.

But even if she came back, when would it be?

If Elika didn't get off the glacier soon, she would freeze for sure.

Chapter
Fourteen

It was after 11 p.m. when the sun finally set. The sky turned pink and orange and threw rainbow colors over the walls of the ice cave. Elika alternated jumping jacks to keep warm with sleeping curled up in the leaf garment. Though she was tired, she couldn't sleep deeply. She was too cold, and felt on edge.

Aunt Caroline had been officially gone for over twelve hours. And her phone battery was almost dead.

Elika's eyes adjusted to the dim light in the cave. Without the sun, she could only see in black and white. The giant was a big, shadowy shape sitting in the corner of the cave.

The giant didn't need sleep. She only meditated for rest. Whenever Elika tried to slip by her, she came out of meditation and talked with Elika.

Escape wasn't looking likely.

Besides being cold and the prisoner of the Ice Giant, Elika had another problem. She was hungry. Starving. The only thing she had eaten all day was the half chocolate bar she found in her jacket pocket, and that was long ago.

Elika couldn't share food with the giant. The giant ate ice. She took huge chunks out of the wall and crunched them. The giant offered to catch Elika a rabbit or fox, but Elika couldn't imagine trying to eat one of those poor creatures raw. Besides, she had always been vegetarian. Even a cooked furry creature would be hard to eat.

Her stomach cramped with hunger as she thought of the hot bowl of pasta at the hotel. She would give anything to be in that hotel right now, eating dinner.

A pang of loneliness made her eyes tear as she remembered eating dinner with Aunt Caroline. She couldn't believe it. She actually missed her weird aunt.

Elika rubbed the tears away. It wasn't time for

feeling sad. It was time for action. She wasn't going to get any closer to that nice bowl of pasta by waiting here.

As she lay in the leaf garment waiting for sunrise, she thought of a plan. It wasn't a plan, exactly. It was more of a way to convince the giant to let her go.

Elika had no idea where she was. If she could escape, she would still be lost on the glacier. Still, it was better than staying in the ice cave.

Once sunrise came, coloring the cave with pink and orange light, Elika stood up from the leaf garment and stretched. The giant came out of her crossed-leg position to talk to her, and Elika tried her plan.

"So, when you assumed I wasn't engaged or betrothed, I think you said?" Elika said. "I didn't want Aunt Caroline to know, so I didn't say anything. I am secretly married. To Henry."

"Henry?"

"He's French."

"*Je parle Francais*," the Ice Giant said. "I speak French."

"*Je parle alcun paroles*," Elika said. "I speak

some words."

"*Je parle tout le langue*," the Ice Giant said, looking proud.

"You speak all languages?" Elika said, almost forgetting her plan in amazement. "All of them in the world?"

"No, just the ones that have come to this land, which you call Iceland," the Giant said. "French, English, Danish, Swedish, German, of course the language of the Ice People, and Icelandic too. You speak Icelandic?"

"No, but my Mom does," Elika said. "She's from here."

Elika went back to her plan.

"Anyway, I miss Henry very much," she said. "I would like to bring him here."

The Ice Giant thought for awhile.

"I am sorry. I know what it's like to lose a husband. How long have you been together?"

"Three years," Elika said. It would mean they got married at ten years old. But she hoped the giant wouldn't know how weird that was.

"That is not so long," the giant said. "I think you

will be OK without him. And I've been thinking..."

"Thinking?" Elika said, disappointed that her plan wasn't working.

"There is another ice cave near a geyser. So you will be warm. You can soak in a natural hot spring there. You won't have to keep jumping up and down."

It actually sounded tempting. She would love to soak in a natural hot spring right now.

"But Aunt Caroline is coming back," Elika said. "She won't be able to find us if we move from here."

Maybe Aunt Caroline was taking so long because she had gotten lost. Elika could only hope she was coming back for her. She had promised, after all.

"An even better reason to go," the Ice Giant said. "I don't like her."

"Um…"

"We will go now," the Ice Giant said.

Elika sadly got to her feet. Her plan had gone all wrong. Now they were leaving the cave, and even if Aunt Caroline came back, she wouldn't find Elika.

The Ice Giant took the leaf garment off the floor and pulled it over her enormous body. Once it was on, Elika could see it was a big cloak with a hood.

Suddenly, the giant turned sharply to Elika. Her eyes looked fierce.

"Humans don't marry at ten," the Ice Giant said in a grating voice. "Why are you tricking me?"

"Oh, I...I'm sorry," Elika said. "You're right, it isn't nice to trick people—or giants. It's just that I'm hungry and cold. I want to go home. And I do like Henry."

"The one who joked about the ice skates?" the giant said.

Elika nodded yes.

"And you like him so much you are learning French?"

Elika nodded again.

"I don't like this Henry," the Ice Giant said. "He jokes about your ancestor's beautiful land, which is not all ice. He takes you away from learning your people's language."

Elika was struck dumb.

"You will have a better life with me," the Ice Giant said. "I will teach you Icelandic."

The Ice Giant suddenly sounded like her mom.

Elika had the weird feeling her mom would agree with her.

Except, of course, Mom wouldn't agree about living in an ice cave.

Elika had to come up with a better plan, so she could escape and find Aunt Caroline again.

But her mind went blank.

The Ice Giant stared expectantly at her.

She had run out of time.

Chapter
Fifteen

The giant was intent on leaving immediately. Elika, panicked, looked around for some way to leave Aunt Caroline a message. But she didn't know where they were going, so she couldn't exactly draw a map in the snow or anything.

"Coming?" the Ice Giant said.

Elika sat on the ice floor. It was much colder without the leaf garment, but she didn't want to leave when there was still a chance Aunt Caroline would find them.

"No," Elika said. "I want to wait for Aunt Caroline."

"She's not coming," the Ice Giant said. "She left yesterday, and a whole nighttime has passed."

Elika's heart sank.

"It will be warm for you in the hot spring," the giant said. "It's not far."

Elika reluctantly got up. Her legs were almost frozen. It would be amazing to soak in a hot spring.

Maybe she could leave a trail, Elika thought. She could purposefully stamp in the snow to leave her footprints as clearly as possible as they walked.

She shuffled through the tunnel, following the giant.

When she exited the cave, the bright light of day blinded her. So she couldn't see why the Ice Giant made an ice-cracking, terrible roar.

Before Elika's sight came back, she was hugged by something that knocked the breath out of her. Her heart warmed when she realized it was person-shaped.

"Aunt Caroline?" Elika said, hugging the warm human back. "Is that you?"

"Elika!" Aunt Caroline said. "I'm so sorry I took so long. I brought help."

Elika turned, blinking to clear her vision. An angry-looking couple held two flaming torches. A third woman who looked as old as her grandmother pointed a rifle at the Ice Giant.

The Ice Giant roared. She backed away.

"Let us take Elika," Aunt Caroline said to the giant. "Let her return home with us, and we won't hurt you."

The Ice Giant stamped her feet with frustration.

Elika fell onto her knees as the icy earth shook. The couple and old woman linked arms to stay standing, and held the fiery torches nearer to the giant.

The Ice Giant took a big step back towards the cave.

She turned two big, sad eyes to Elika.

"I will be alone," she wailed. Great snowflakes fell from her eyes. They formed two piles by the giant's huge feet.

"Snowflake tears," Aunt Caroline said, holding up her phone to take a picture. "How wonderful."

"Aunt Caroline," Elika said. "We can't just leave her all alone."

"But isn't this what you wanted?" Aunt Caroline said. "Don't you want to go home?"

"I'm not saying I want to stay here in the ice cave," Elika said. "But I don't feel good about leaving her all alone. There aren't any other giants here."

The Ice Giant rubbed her eyes, breaking snowflakes across her cheeks. She turned to Elika.

"I will come with you to your home," the Ice Giant said. "Even if she is there." She pointed to Aunt Caroline.

Elika had a moment of panic, trying to imagine the giant living in their backyard in New York. There was no way she would fit in their house. None of her friends would ever dare to come over again.

"Well, not New York, no," Elika said. "You'd melt there."

The couple with the torches came closer to the Ice Giant, who backed into the cave.

"These torches will not burn forever," the woman said. "We should leave now."

"No," the Ice Giant said. "Please do not go." She turned wide eyes to Elika.

Elika felt a pain in her heart. She just couldn't leave the Ice Giant all alone.

But she couldn't live in the ice cave either.

There must be another solution. But what was it?

Elika didn't know.

Chapter
Sixteen

The three Icelanders threatened the Ice Giant. But Elika didn't want to leave anymore. She wanted to help.

"We can't just leave her there, all lonely," Elika said.

Aunt Caroline sighed deeply.

"You're right, Elika," Aunt Caroline said. "We have a little time before the torches burn out. Let's call a truce for the moment and discuss Elika's idea."

"Truce," the Ice Giant said. "Yes, I know that word. We will have a peaceful discussion, with no fires."

The Icelandic couple backed away from the giant and crouched down to rest. But the old woman came closer to the giant.

"Giants," the older woman said, and pointed her rifle at the giant. "They have always made trouble.

This is our land, not yours!"

"Mom," the man with the torch said. "Please lower the gun. This giant seems reasonable at least."

The grandmother made a harrumph noise, but sat down and lowered the gun, at least partway. She kept her eyes on the giant.

"These are friends of my colleague, Edmund," Aunt Caroline told Elika. "You know, Edmund is the one who left us the crampons and jackets."

"How did they get here?" Elika asked.

"I did a lot of texting," Aunt Caroline said. "Edmund gave me their address and I drove out to their house. That's why it took so long."

"Well, I'm so glad you came," Elika said. "We were just about to change caves."

"We should have gone earlier," the Ice Giant mumbled to herself.

Aunt Caroline put a protective arm around Elika's shoulder.

"So, what is your idea, Elika?" Aunt Caroline asked. The Ice Giant leaned towards them from the cave to hear.

Elika told them her plan, which was, Elika had to

admit, slightly crazy.

Elika's plan involved the Ice Giant going to the Himalayas and meeting the Amber Giant. Elika had no idea if they would get along. But at least they were both giants.

When she was finished, neither Aunt Caroline or the giant seemed to know what to say. They stared at Elika with blank faces.

"So," Elika said after a long silence. "What do you think about my idea?"

"You are saying I should move to the mountains in this faraway country, Nepal?" the Ice Giant said. "But I have always lived in this land. For 350 years my feet have known this ice."

"Isn't it time for a change, then?" Elika said.

The Ice Giant shook her big head.

"You are young," she said. "You do not know what it is to leave one's homeland."

Aunt Caroline was thinking more practically. She took out her journal and sketched a flowchart and an airplane.

"Let's say the Ice Giant did want to go to Nepal," Aunt Caroline said, tapping the page with her pen.

"How could we get her there? I don't think we have a plane big enough, and even if we did, I'm not sure we could keep it at a freezing temperature."

"Maybe by ship?" Elika said.

Aunt Caroline nodded.

"It would take longer," Aunt Caroline said. "And we'd need to move her to a truck once we hit land. But yes, it may be more workable than an airplane." She made more notes.

The Ice Giant was quiet for a long time. Then she turned to Elika.

"I might come," she said. "But I need to talk with you. Privately." She gave Aunt Caroline a fierce look.

"No way," Aunt Caroline said. "The kid sticks with me."

"Then I will not go," the Ice Giant said. "And I will moan in Elika's dreams as before."

Elika felt her face go pale. She really didn't want to dream all those horribly lonely dreams. She'd never be able to sleep again.

"OK, you can talk to me," Elika said. "But you have to promise not to try to steal me."

The Ice Giant stared at her.

"You will only come with me into the cave if I promise?" the giant said.

Elika nodded, trying to look confident.

"I would not make a promise with a human," the Ice Giant said. "Except for you. I will make the ice promise."

The Ice Giant closed her eyes and breathed very deeply. Her ice blue body turned pink.

Elika watched, amazed, as the Ice Giant mumbled some words including Elika's name.

Then the giant opened her eyes and went back to her normal color. She lifted her foot. There, inside her foot, was writing in the ice. It said, 'I will not steal Elika'.

Elika was speechless.

"So you will come speak with me in the cave?" the Ice Giant said.

Elika's heart pounded. She was afraid of being alone with the Ice Giant. But she had to trust her after the ice promise.

"Yes, OK," Elika said.

"No way!" Aunt Caroline said. The Icelanders jumped off the rocks and came towards the giant angrily, waving the torches and pointing the rifle.

"Didn't you see the ice promise?" Elika said, standing in front of the Ice Giant to protect her from the fire. "I trust her, after that."

The Ice Giant blinked, and a warm smile stretched across her face.

"Thank you," she said.

"The ice promise was something special," Aunt Caroline said. "And creatures like giants are strongly bound by promises in magical ways."

Aunt Caroline chewed her lip as she thought.

"If you're sure, Elika, I'll let you go with the giant alone," Aunt Caroline said. "But if anything strange happens, call out. I will enter the cave in five minutes whether or not I hear from you."

"I need fifteen minutes," the Ice Giant said, her expression cold.

"We can give you fifteen," Elika said. "Right, Aunt Caroline?"

"Fifteen and not a second longer," Aunt Caroline said.

"Silly human time-keeping," the Ice Giant mumbled, and beckoned Elika into the cave.

Elika squeezed Aunt Caroline's hand.

"It will be OK," Elika said, sounding more confident than she felt. She followed the Ice Giant back into the cave.

Could she trust the Ice Giant?

Or was she making a huge mistake?

Chapter
Seventeen

Elika followed the Ice Giant back into the cave, through the tunnel of ice, all the way into the big chamber. Walking with crampons on was easier now, but she still had to go slow. It was a relief to sit on the solid ice floor once they reached the big room with the moon-and-stars ceiling.

The Ice Giant sat cross-legged next to Elika. Her expression softened, and her smile returned.

"Just like old times," the giant said, as Elika wrapped the leaf garment around herself.

It would have been funny, except Elika had actually never wanted to see this room again after her long imprisonment. In fact, what the giant said was a little scary.

"Thank you for helping me," the Ice Giant said. "You could have left me and gone back home."

"I'm sorry those people attacked you with the torches," Elika said. "The truth is, though I don't want to live here, and I do want to go home to my family, I'm still your friend."

"Are you angry that I stole you before?" the Ice Giant said. She held up her foot. 'I will not steal Elika' was still written inside.

"Yes, a little," Elika said. "But yesterday when I thought maybe I'd never see another human again, I felt so lonely. I think without other giants around, you're too sad, and it made you…well, desperate."

"So you really think I should go to these Himalayas?" the Ice Giant said.

"I think you need some giant company," Elika said.

"I cannot find my people in the North," the Ice Giant explained. "Even if I did find them, without my husband, I would not know my place with them."

"Well, at least there would be one giant to be your friend in the Himalayas," Elika said.

"In our story, the People of the Yak are very strong," the Ice Giant said. "Is that what the Amber Giant is like?"

"He is strong," Elika said. "And he's friendly. He is kind of a hero. He saves humans from avalanches and stuff."

"Hmm," the giant said, looking concerned. "This does not sound like a giant I would understand. Why would he save humans?"

Elika shrugged.

"Humans are happy about it."

"Well, is he handsome?"

Elika thought about it. The Amber Giant was covered in hair, and the Ice Giant had no hair at all. She didn't know how the Ice Giant would feel about hair. She wouldn't mention that.

"He's a nice color."

"How old is he?"

"Well, let's see. He was asleep for 1,000 years. Before that, he was 123 years old. Aunt Caroline found him thirty years ago. So he's either 1,153 years old or just 153."

"153! So young," the Ice Giant said. "He is much younger than me—less than half my age."

"But he's older," Elika said, trying to convince the Ice Giant to like him.

"He's actually 1,153 years old," Elika said. "He could tell you about the ancient past."

The Ice Giant stared at Elika. "I have nothing to lose," the giant finally said. "I cannot stay here."

"So you'll come?" Elika said and clapped her hands.

"OK, I will do it," the giant said. "But I will not go in Caroline's human-mover."

The Ice Giant stood up to her incredibly tall height. She went to the corner of the cave and lifted her arm up to the high, vaulted ceiling. She took a beautiful goblet from a hole in the ice there.

"The Ice Chalice," the Ice Giant said, showing Elika the goblet. Three strands of ice were woven together, forming the stem. The ice cup at the top looked like a flower opening. It was beautiful.

"It is magic, and very old," the Ice Giant said. "Older than me. I have only seen it used once in all my 350 years."

"Wow," Elika said. "What does it do?" She wanted to touch it, but was afraid to break it.

"If I drink from this," the Ice Giant said. "I will be transported to my heart's desire."

"What is your heart's desire?" she asked.

"I desire to find another giant, but I haven't met the Amber Giant, so he cannot be my heart's desire," the Ice Giant said. "I can be transported to you. You must be in the Himalayas when I drink this. I will be transported to where you are, and if it is not in the snowy mountains, I will melt."

"Me?" Elika said. "I'm your heart's desire? But why do you love me so much?"

"Ah, young one," the Ice Giant said. "Love is not explainable. But if I had to say a reason, it could be because you are my first human friend. Actually, you are my first friend, giant or human, in a long time. Also, you brought me the gift."

"It's just a pretty rock," Elika said. "A quartz crystal, I mean."

"It's a healing stone," the Ice Giant said. "Did you not know? It heals us creatures of ice."

"Why don't you use it?" Elika asked.

The giant smiled at her.

"I am not sick, young one," the Ice Giant said. "I am strong and healthy."

"But you're sad," Elika said. "Can you use it on

your broken heart?"

The Ice Giant stared at her wordlessly. Then she went to the corner of the cave and pulled the crystal out of its hiding place by the conch shell. She held it to her heart.

"Crystal, heal my lonely heart," she said. The crystal glowed pink. It shimmered and melted. It disappeared into the giant's chest.

"It is better," the Ice Giant said. She took a long breath in. "Yes, my heart is happier."

"I feel healed, but I have not forgotten him," the Ice Giant said.

"Who?" Elika asked.

"My husband," the giant answered. She showed Elika her leg. Deep inside were the strange symbols of her husband's name.

"My ice promise when I married him was to love him always."

"So you still love him," Elika said.

"Yes, but now it does not hurt," the Ice Giant said, holding her heart with her icy hand. "Ah my human friend, you have helped me so much."

"Elika!" Aunt Caroline's voice came through the

cave. The noise of crunching crampons followed. Her aunt was coming to find her.

"If you don't come out right now, my friends with the torches are coming in!" Aunt Caroline said.

"Coming!" Elika called down the long tunnel. "Our fifteen minutes are up," she said to the giant. "Let's go tell her the plan."

"Thank you for trusting me," the Ice Giant said. "So we could speak, just us two."

Elika nodded.

"Thank you for trusting me," Elika said. "How do you know I will be in the Himalayas when you drink from the chalice? It is risky."

"Do you promise to be there?" the Ice Giant asked.

"Yes," Elika said. "A promise is written in the heart."

The Ice Giant looked surprised.

"We say something like that in the Ice People language," the Ice Giant said. "I think you are sometimes wise, young Elika."

"If I could make an ice promise, I would," Elika said. "I can only make an ink promise."

"An ink promise?" the Ice Giant asked.

"I'll show you when we're outside," Elika said.

"Your word is enough," the giant said. "I look in your eyes, Elika, and I have complete faith in you."

Elika felt a glow of pride and honor sweep through her.

As she walked through the ice tunnel, though, the proud feeling left Elika. Instead, uncertain thoughts swirled through her mind. The Ice Giant had faith in her. But could Elika really do it?

What if her parents said she couldn't go?

What if she tried to take a flight and all the airports closed?

What if they got to the Himalayas and couldn't find the Amber Giant?

Elika shook herself of these thoughts.

The plan was set. There was no turning back.

Chapter
Eighteen

Elika found Aunt Caroline in the tunnel. Elika was relieved to see her. Aunt Caroline gave Elika a big hug as they exited the cave together.

Even though Elika mostly trusted the giant, a small part of her had wondered if the giant would steal her after all. So it was a relief to be outside in the bright sunlight.

The three Icelanders with the torches and rifles came towards the giant, but Elika stood in front of them and asked them to sit down again.

"Look, we have a plan," Elika said. "The giant is our friend."

"So, will she come meet Amby?" Aunt Caroline said. "All the way in the Himalayas? I have been thinking about a possible compartment to ship her there…"

"I will go," the Ice Giant said. "But I will not go in your compartment."

"She has her own way there," Elika said. "A magic way."

When Elika told Aunt Caroline about the ice chalice, she wanted to see it immediately. But the Ice Giant said no.

"Elika is the only one who can know my giant secrets," she said. "I will not show you."

Aunt Caroline begged to see it, but the Ice Giant was firm.

"Elika is my only human friend," the Ice Giant said, and gave Aunt Caroline a scary look.

"Aunt Caroline," Elika said. "I told her I would be in the Himalayas in five days. Can you take me to the Amber Giant?"

"Of course," Aunt Caroline said. "I always wanted you to meet him."

"OK," Elika said to the Ice Giant. "I will see you soon, in the mountains." She wrote her promise on her hand: *I will be in the Himalayas for the Ice Giant.*

"An ink promise," the giant said. "I have never seen that. How wonderful."

The Ice Giant took a long look at Elika, then went back into the cave.

Relief filled Elika. She was really, truly free to go home now.

They had to hike back to the car first. Though it was downhill and Elika wore her normal shoes instead of the wobbly crampons, it was still exhausting. Elika went slowly. Waves of hunger washed through her.

When they got to the cars, Aunt Caroline thanked her colleagues' friends, and Elika curled up in the passenger's seat. She fell asleep, finally feeling warm.

When she woke up, they were at the hotel in Hofn. They went straight to the hotel restaurant for dinner.

"The pasta!" Elika ordered with pure happiness. All she wanted was a hot, steaming dinner, a hot, steaming shower, and then sleep.

As they ate, Aunt Caroline wanted to hear all about the ice cave and if Elika saw any other magical items there. But Elika was too tired and hungry.

"Later," Elika said, in between mouthfuls of the

pasta. "Everything later. I am too hungry to even talk."

After dinner, Elika took a long, hot shower and enjoyed the steam that enveloped her. It was much nicer than the freezing cold air of an ice cave. Feeling clean and happily full, she went to bed.

When she woke up, she looked at the clock and got a shock—10 a.m. She had slept for twelve whole hours. But hadn't Aunt Caroline said she would wake her up at 9 a.m. for breakfast?

Rubbing her sleepy eyes, Elika threw open the curtains. What she saw clenched her stomach with nervousness.

Where was the mountain?

All she could see was white.

When she knocked on Aunt Caroline's door, her aunt explained she had been awake for a few hours, but decided to let Elika sleep since there was no driving in the weather conditions. They walked down to the hotel restaurant for breakfast.

"A snowstorm," Aunt Caroline said over coffee.

"A snowstorm in July?" Elika asked, drinking hot chocolate. She had ordered toast, but the snowstorm was making her too nervous to eat.

"The locals here say it's unusual, but that it can happen," Aunt Caroline said.

"When can we get to the airport?" Elika asked, her stomach clenching with fear. "We have to be in the Himalayas in only four days!"

Aunt Caroline didn't seem worried. She took a long sip of her coffee.

"We'll get there, we have plenty of time," she said. "The storm will probably blow over by tomorrow."

Elika put her toast down. Her throat felt too tight to eat anymore. She spent the rest of the day napping, explaining to her parents why she had to be in the Himalayas soon, and staring out at the white sky.

The next morning looked equally as white.

Now even Aunt Caroline was nervous.

"We can't reach the Ice Giant to tell her not to drink from the ice chalice," Aunt Caroline said over another hotel meal. "There is no way to drive in this storm, much less hike into the glacier."

Elika pulled her dark ponytail.

"If we stay here, she'll transport into the hotel

when she drinks from the chalice," Elika said, shivering as she imagined the destruction she could cause.

"She'd smash through the ceiling and probably hurt herself," Aunt Caroline said, "and maybe some of the hotel guests."

"I can't wait outside in the freezing cold just waiting for her to transport to me," Elika said.

Aunt Caroline agreed that the best thing was to go to Kathmandu if at all possible. But the latest flight they could catch to be in the Himalayas in time would be the next day.

Any later, and the Ice Giant might teleport onto the flying plane.

And crash it.

Elika shivered. She wanted to be hopeful. But deep down, she wondered if the plan was too crazy to work.

It could be a disaster.

At midnight, Aunt Caroline pounded on Elika's door. Elika sleepily dragged herself to open it. She jolted awake when she saw her aunt with her suitcase.

"The storm just cleared!" Aunt Caroline said, her eyes bright. "Let's go now. We can make the flight if we start driving now."

New hope filled Elika with energy. She threw her things in the suitcase and followed Aunt Caroline into the night. The sky was painted amber and gold, the sun a low, molten disk on the horizon.

"Sunset at midnight," Elika said. "It looks like a honey sky."

Aunt Caroline gave her a sideways smile.

"There is that poetry again, Elika," she said.

For some reason this time it didn't bother Elika. Maybe poetry was weird, but it was a good kind of weird.

Though the drive was beautiful, with the painted sky and the early rising of the sun, they were both nervous about missing the flight. Aunt Caroline drove faster than she ever had.

"Hopefully they don't have traffic cops on the road!" her aunt said, grinning.

Elika could swear her crazy aunt was having fun.

They made it to the airport in time for the flight. In fact, they had plenty of time. The flight was delayed two hours.

"Let's hope the Ice Giant isn't early," Aunt Caroline said, echoing Elika's thoughts. But unlike Elika, who felt sick with nerves, her aunt was grinning.

"I love adventures, don't you?" her aunt said.

Elika shook her head no.

Her aunt gave her a hug.

"Don't worry, it will be fine," her aunt said. "You'll see. We'll make it in time."

Elika wished she shared her aunt's hopefulness.

She was tense during the whole flight.

Chapter
Nineteen

They landed without the Ice Giant appearing, and Elika felt deeply relieved. But she felt stressed again when they got to the city.

Elika took her first steps in Kathmandu, Nepal. Everything was unfamiliar and she felt dizzy from all the new sights, sounds and smells. Another thought made her feel worse. It was hot.

If the Ice Giant teleported now, she would melt for sure.

A rickshaw, a carriage pulled by a bicycle, rattled by. Elika felt a whoosh of wind as she stepped back onto the sidewalk.

"It's so crazy here!" Elika said, eyeing the stream of traffic in front of her. Cars, buses, motor scooters, rickshaws, bicycles and pedestrians shared the road. It was chaos.

A million smells filled her senses, she couldn't even distinguish them. Sweat, fried dumplings, chili, she thought as they hurried down the uneven sidewalk to meet Caroline's Sherpa friend Mike.

She stared at a yak being led down the street. It had on a heavy pack, and the bells on its harness jingled.

Aunt Caroline didn't seem to even notice the yak. She walked quickly through the narrow streets. Elika struggled to keep up.

"I can't even keep up with you on the sidewalks," Elika said. "How am I going to hike into the mountains?"

"Oh, Sherpa Mike and I agreed you aren't ready for a strenuous hike up into the high Himalayas," Aunt Caroline explained. "We're going to take a helicopter into the mountains. Besides, there isn't time to hike up. The Ice Giant could appear soon."

Elika had never been in a helicopter. She felt afraid at the thought of going in one. But another thought made her more nervous.

"What if she teleports while we're flying?" Elika said.

"We better be quick," Aunt Caroline said, and winked at Elika.

They picked up their pace and hurried down the sidewalk.

"Are helicopters really noisy?" Elika said, craning her neck to look at the colorful flags hung above the street. Aunt Caroline said they were prayer flags. They fluttered in the wind.

Elika looked in front of her just in time to dodge an old woman in a colorful dress. The woman was moving fast and almost smacked into her.

"We'll have headphones to make the helicopter less noisy," Aunt Caroline said. "Don't worry, it'll all be fine."

Elika was panting by the time they stopped at a corner. Sherpa Mike, who was an old Nepalese man with silver hair and beard, introduced himself. Another friend of Aunt Caroline's walked down the street to meet them. It turned out to be Edmund, Aunt Caroline's colleague.

"Thank you so much for everything," Elika said to Edmund. "The ski jacket, the crampons, and sending your friends to rescue me from the Ice

Giant's cave. I think you saved my life."

Edmund grinned, his round cheeks red.

"Congratulations to you," he said. "Not many have met an Ice Giant and survived the experience."

Elika felt nervous. What could she say to this person that helped her so much?

"Well," she said. "The chocolate bar in the pocket of that ski jacket was all I had to eat one day. You helped a lot."

Edmund shrugged, though he smiled bigger.

"I would do anything for your Aunt Caroline," he said, and smiled at her aunt.

"Let's get going," Aunt Caroline said, smiling back at him.

They piled into Sherpa Mike's truck. But just before Elika climbed in, she paused.

A snowstorm seemed to be forming on the sidewalk.

A snowstorm? In Kathmandu, in July?

But it was way too hot for snow. Elika was sweating from their hurried journey through the city, and she had stripped down to a t-shirt.

Her heart sank when the snowstorm contracted

into a dense cloud that formed arms, legs and a head. The Ice Giant took shape.

"We're too late!" Elika yelled.

The enormous Ice Giant was standing in front of them. And the sun was beating down on her unprotected head.

The Ice Giant fixed her blue eyes on Elika's. At first she looked happy, but her smile quickly turned to a frown.

"The sun, it is so strong," the Ice Giant said, covering her head with her ice hands. "Where are we?"

"Kathmandu," Elika said sadly. "I'm so sorry, we are late."

The hot sun blazed down. Water already covered the Ice Giant in a film.

"Run into the mountains!" Aunt Caroline said, jumping out of the truck. "It's colder up there."

"I feel too weak," the Ice Giant said. "The ice chalice, it made me feel weak, and now this awful heat."

Elika looked around frantically for a solution. But she couldn't see one. The giant was way too big to fit into any of the air-conditioned shops.

A scream rang out. A lady in an "I Love Nepal" t-shirt clutched her heart with fear. Other tourists gathered around, some shaking with fear and some snapping pictures.

"What is it?" someone shouted. "It looks dangerous!"

Sherpa Mike stood in front of the giant and put his hands up in a calming gesture.

"She is a giant, and giants are friends to us," he said.

A Nepalese woman in a sari came and stood by him. Three children in colorful outfits joined them. Soon there was a group standing in front of the Ice Giant, protecting her.

The crowd of tourists grew bigger too. One picked up a stone and threatened to throw it at the giant.

"No," Sherpa Mike said to him. "The Amber Giant has saved many lives. I tell you, giants are our friends."

"She's sick," Elika yelled out to the group. The Ice Giant crouched down, trying to cover her head with her arms. Already, a puddle of water formed on the pavement.

The Ice Giant met Elika's eyes again.

"I am not sick," the Ice Giant said. "I am melting." Snowflake tears formed in her eyes and quickly turned to water.

Despite the heat, goosebumps covered Elika's arms.

The Ice Giant could die.

But what could she do?

The Ice Giant was getting thinner, right in front of the crowd. Everyone was silent, including the tourists.

Suddenly, there was a lot of noise across the street. A group of people were hauling huge, black machines from a ski shop.

"Before we had those fancy snow machines, we had old fashioned ice chippers," one of the strong-looking skiers said to Elika.

They set up three machines around the giant, and turned them on. They fed bag after bag of ice into the machines, and ice chips flew out the other end. Soon the Ice Giant was covered in a mist of ice.

Elika couldn't see her anymore.

"Ice Giant!" Elika yelled into the ice mist. "How do you feel?"

"Better," the Ice Giant said in a strong voice. "I am not melting and I am not hot!"

"Problem is, we're going to run out of ice at this rate," one of the skiers said.

"We can't just stay here forever, covering her in ice," another skier said, agreeing.

Aunt Caroline spoke with the skiers, showing them her sketch pad. She must have an idea. Elika hoped it was a good one.

"Do you think the Ice Giant would hold two machines over her head, one with each hand?" Aunt Caroline asked Elika. "Two skiers volunteered to keep feeding the ice in the machines while she runs into the mountains."

Elika's eyes widened with awe at the skiers. It would be dangerous for them to be so high up, in the hands of a running giant. But she couldn't think of another way to save the Ice Giant.

Elika yelled the idea into the ice mist.

"I don't trust humans!" the Ice Giant yelled back.

"But you have to," Elika said. "Or the ice will run out and then you will melt."

"We will trust you with our lives, and you will trust us with yours," one of the skiers yelled into the ice mist.

After a few minutes of silence, an "OK" came out of the ice mist.

The Ice Giant had agreed.

The courageous skiers pushed the big machines into the ice mist. Elika couldn't believe how brave they were.

A minute later, the Ice Giant stood up, a machine and a human in each hand. She raised her hands up so the ice chips formed a cloud around her head.

Elika could see her body was thin from melting. The ice chips were protecting her head and shoulders, but her legs and feet were hot and melting.

"Run!" Elika yelled up towards the Ice Giant's head. "Run, but please don't hurt the people!"

The Ice Giant ran towards the mountains.

Elika watched her go, a huge giant with an ice mist around her head.

"Don't worry, Elika," Aunt Caroline said and winked. "The craziest ideas are usually the ones to work. Now let's get to the helipad and follow them."

Chapter
Twenty

The helicopter was parked at the helipad a mile away. The drive there seemed to take forever, with all the traffic. They got stuck behind a slow-moving yak for a good fifteen minutes before they could pass it.

When they arrived, Elika leapt out of the car and piled into the helicopter along with Aunt Caroline, Sherpa Mike and Edmund. Though it was a tiny space, and the whirring blades of the helicopter made a terrible noise, there was no time to be afraid.

As they lifted off, Elika focused on finding the Ice Giant. They flew over the busy city and soon reached rockier places with fewer people.

Small huts dotted the foothills below. They didn't see any sign of the Ice Giant until they were pretty high up in the mountains. Then, it was obvious where she had been.

Rivers of snow cascaded down the mountain.

"Snow and rock falls down the mountain. These are avalanches," Sherpa Mike said. "The Ice Giant's great strides create them."

Elika couldn't believe the Ice Giant could cause avalanches just by running. Then she saw a great figure with a cloud of ice covering its head.

"There she is!" Elika shouted, pointing out the window. "What is that…three o'clock? Just to the right!"

Her stomach lurched as Sherpa Mike redirected the helicopter towards the running figure. She hoped the people who powered the ice chippers were OK. They must be freezing in her ice hands.

"I'll get in front of the Ice Giant," Sherpa Mike said. "Then we can lead her to her new home."

Once the helicopter got close, the Ice Giant stopped running.

The cloud of ice chips cleared.

Enormous blue eyes stared at the helicopter.

Elika hoped the giant realized her friends were

inside. What if the giant thought the helicopter was an enormous mosquito?

The humans on her hands jumped up and down, waving hello. To Elika's relief, the Ice Giant nodded her head in greeting.

Sherpa Mike flew away, leading the Ice Giant higher up into the mountains. They went slow, so as not to cause any more avalanches. It became cloudy, and Elika was relived the Ice Giant wouldn't have to worry about the sun all the way up here.

Elika stared at the empty landscape below her. There was only snow, rock, and the gray water of a lake that reflected the cloudy sky. Sherpa Mike landed.

"This is where Amby lives," Aunt Caroline said as they left the helicopter. "I can't wait for you to meet him, Elika."

Elika jumped down into the snow, almost losing her balance. She was hit with a wave of cold air. Even the layers of clothing Sherpa Mike had given her, plus the ski jacket couldn't keep the cold out.

The Ice Giant was making her way towards them. Elika felt relieved to see her. She seemed to be walking OK, though she was thin.

But Aunt Caroline was waving at something in the opposite direction.

"There he is!" Aunt Caroline yelled. "Amby, we are here!"

"Master?" a low, excited voice came from the distance.

Then Elika saw him. The Amber Giant.

She gasped and her heart raced.

He was both bigger and hairier than she expected.

And she could smell him from here. She wrinkled her nose.

"Elika," said a high, clear voice close to her. She turned. The Ice Giant lowered the two humans carefully onto the snow, and crouched down to look Elika in the eye. The giant smiled a warm smile.

"How are you?" Elika asked, smiling back.

"I am well," the Ice Giant said. "Thinner than normal. I will need to eat a lot of ice to gain back what melted away."

"I'm so glad you didn't melt away," Elika said.

"Thank you," the Ice Giant said. "You kept your

ink promise. I am alive, in the mountains. And I have new friends." The Ice Giant smiled at the two people from the ski shop who had powered the ice machine. They were jumping up and down, trying to get warm. Sherpa Mike was giving them something from a thermos. Elika bet it was yak butter tea.

"You're very welcome," one of the skiers said, her teeth chattering with cold. "It's not every day you get to save a giant. I'm Patricia and this is Rick. We're pleased to meet you."

"I am in your debt," the Ice Giant said. "Elika used to be my only human friend. Now you have saved me with a courageous act, and if I can ever repay you, I will." The Ice Giant bowed to them.

"I'm glad you like humans now," Elika said. "And I'm glad you're OK."

"I am OK," the Ice Giant said. "I don't even have a headache, I am just hungry. Thanks to you all."

Elika wrinkled her nose. The very strong smell of the Amber Giant seemed very close to her. She turned to see the Amber Giant standing nearby, next to Aunt Caroline. Her head came to his knee.

"Master," the Amber Giant said, in a low, excited voice. "Is that my new friend?"

At those words, something unexpected happened to the Ice Giant. Her whole ice-body turned red. Her eyes grew fierce.

Elika gasped.

"Are you OK?" Elika asked. "You're all red!"

"I'm angry," the Ice Giant said. "More angry than I have been in centuries." Hail started to fall from the sky.

"Why?" Elika asked. "Why now?"

"Is this giant your slave?" the Ice Giant asked Aunt Caroline.

"Oh no," Aunt Caroline said. "Of course not."

"He called you Master!" the Ice Giant roared.

"Oh, well? OK, I guess I am his Master," Aunt Caroline explained. "But I would never misuse my power. I don't command him."

"Master is my friend," the Amber Giant said.

"Long have the Ice People been slaves to human witches and sorcerers," the Ice Giant said. "Humans who use the Ice People for their own greedy purposes."

Patricia and Rick walked far away from the Ice Giant, along with Sherpa Mike. They watched in horror as the Ice Giant clenched a fist and threatened Aunt Caroline.

Ice chips pelted down from the sky.

"Master," the Amber Giant said and ran in front of Aunt Caroline to protect her.

"Why do you protect the one who enslaved you?" the Ice Giant said.

"Humans are my friends," the Amber Giant said. "We must not hurt humans."

"Maybe some of them are friends," the Ice Giant said. "But I cannot let you stay a slave. You will be free of the spell once I crush her."

The Ice Giant, glowing red, crouched down to Aunt Caroline and raised her ice fist.

Aunt Caroline, who wasn't afraid of anything, gasped.

Elika shut her eyes. She couldn't watch what happened next.

She had never seen anything as scary as the bright red, angry Ice Giant.

Chapter
Twenty-one

Elika didn't dare look. Hail pelted her. She heard a loud growl. She peeked through her fingers, worried about what she might see. She was relieved to see that Aunt Caroline was OK. The Amber Giant stood in front of her, protecting her.

The Amber Giant was growling. He made himself as tall as possible and stamped his feet.

"You think I cannot take you?" the Ice Giant said, raising her fists. "You are shorter than me, and a child compared to my many years."

"You cannot hurt Master," the Amber Giant said. He clenched his hairy fist, and his fangs gleamed sharply.

Aunt Caroline walked under the Amber Giant's legs and stood in front of the Ice Giant with her arms crossed.

"Look, it's true that I accidentally enslaved him," Aunt Caroline said. "But I didn't mean to. I was only eleven. A child!"

"And why have you not released him?" the Ice Giant said.

"I don't know how," Aunt Caroline said.

If her Aunt Caroline could be brave, Elika guessed she could be too.

She took a deep breath for courage and ran over to the Ice Giant.

"Please," Elika said. "Can we all calm down and talk normally? And please make it stop hailing. It's hurting my head."

The Ice Giant looked at Elika with fierce eyes. Then, to Elika's surprise, she took several deep breaths. She turned from bright red to pink. The hail lessened, then stopped altogether.

"I do not want to hurt you, Elika," the giant said. "And I don't want to hurt my new friends, Patricia and Rick. But Caroline keeps one of my kind as a slave!"

Edmund came to stand next to Aunt Caroline, though his legs wobbled with fear.

"Look, if I may say something," Edmund said, his voice shaky. "I think I may know how to release the giant."

"How?" Aunt Caroline looked at him with big eyes.

"When the Amber Giant woke up, long ago you said, 'para en ras', words in an ancient language that mean 'you are bound to me'," Edmund said. "Say 'para ne ras'. It means 'you are unbound from me' in the same language."

"*Para ne ras*, Amby" Aunt Caroline said loudly to the Amber Giant, who was watching the argument with a confused look on his face.

The Amber Giant blinked a few times.

"How do you feel, Amby?" Aunt Caroline asked the Amber Giant.

"I think I feel the same," the Amber Giant said.

The Ice Giant crossed her arms and pulsed red.

"Obviously the spell didn't work," the Ice Giant said. "He is still your slave."

"We don't know that for sure," Aunt Caroline said. How could they tell if the giant was released from the spell?

Elika had an idea.

"If it worked, even if Aunt Caroline commands him, he doesn't have to do it," Elika asked. "Right?"

The Ice Giant nodded.

"So, Aunt Caroline," Elika said. "Tell him to do something he doesn't want to do. Let's see what happens."

"Amby," Aunt Caroline said. "Go take a bath."

The Amber Giant stood still.

"No," the Amber Giant said. "I don't want to."

"It worked!" Elika said. "Would he be able to say that if she was still his master?"

"It does seem he is free," the Ice Giant finally said. She turned pink.

"I'm free?" the Amber Giant said. "No Master? But will you still visit me?" He looked sadly at Aunt Caroline.

"Of course I will," Aunt Caroline said and hugged his furry leg. "We're friends. Even if you never take a bath again."

"I love Master! I mean, Caroline," the Amber Giant said.

"I love you too," Aunt Caroline said.

The Ice Giant watched them. Her fierce expression softened. She turned back to her usual color, ice blue.

"I find it strange that a giant and a human could be friends," the Ice Giant said, watching Aunt Caroline hugging Amby's enormous leg.

Elika thought it was strange too. "Maybe it is strange," she said. "But good strange."

The Ice Giant nodded.

"After all you have done for me, Elika," the Ice Giant said. "We are friends."

Elika nodded, a warm glow in her heart. Once upon a time she didn't want to have anything to do with a giant. Now she felt lucky the Ice Giant was her friend.

The giant put a hand to her head.

"I feel very tired," the Ice Giant said. "I need to rest." She turned to look at the big, hairy giant.

"Amber Giant, I am sorry we met by fighting," the Ice Giant said. "I hope we can be friends. Do you know of a cave where I can rest?"

Elika smiled. Maybe the giants would be friends. Then neither of them would feel so lonely.

But it turned out there was no time for the Ice Giant to rest.

A roar sounded, and Elika turned to look for the source of the loud noise. A huge river of snow was heading their way, and the ground began to shake. Her stomach clenched with fear.

It was an avalanche.

Chapter
Twenty-two

The argument between the Ice Giant and Amber Giant had started an avalanche. A white river of snow crashed down the mountain, heading straight for the group. The giants were tall and strong enough to keep standing. But Elika could see the humans would be buried in the snow, or even swept off the mountain.

There was no time to lose. The Amber Giant swept Aunt Caroline, Edmund and Sherpa Mike up in his enormous hands.

"Save the other humans!" the Amber Giant yelled to the Ice Giant.

The Ice Giant scooped Elika, Patricia and Rick up. Elika immediately felt frozen in the ice hands. She huddled together with the other humans, not caring that she didn't know them, just to get warm.

As the Ice Giant ran, Elika bumped along in the ice cave formed by the giant's hands. She was relieved when she was placed gently down in the snow. Her head spun and she had to take deep breaths before the world looked normal again.

The Ice Giant looked at her, worried.

"You are too cold," the Ice Giant said. "You all are," she said, examining Patricia and Rick, who had blue lips. "And your people-carrier is destroyed."

"You saved us!" Elika said. "That warms my heart."

The Ice Giant placed her own hand to her heart and looked thoughtful.

Loud steps echoed off the mountains, and the Amber Giant arrived. He put down the humans, and Elika ran to Aunt Caroline and hugged her.

"You're freezing!" Aunt Caroline said, rubbing Elika's arms.

"You smell!" Elika said. She wasn't kidding. Aunt Caroline smelled like the big, hairy giant.

Though half the people were smelly, and half freezing cold, everyone was alive.

"The Ice Giant is a hero," the Amber Giant said.

"She saves humans, like me."

The Ice Giant smiled, her eyes soft.

"How do you feel?" Elika asked the Ice Giant.

"My heart is warm," the Ice Giant said. "I finally understand why the Amber Giant saves humans. I feel better than before."

"We appreciate it," Patricia said as she drank a cup of Sherpa Mike's thick yak butter tea. "You saved our lives. Thank you."

"I think I will help the Amber Giant to save humans," the Ice Giant said. "I can learn much from this young giant."

The Amber Giant gave her a toothy grin.

"Is she our friend now?" the Amber Giant asked Aunt Caroline.

"Yes, Amby," Aunt Caroline said.

The Amber Giant ran up to the Ice Giant. "Let's find some caves."

"I do need to find a cave to rest in," the Ice Giant said. "Yes, I will go with you."

Elika looked down the mountain. She couldn't even see Kathmandu. It would be a very long hike down.

"We're not set up to hike to the city," Aunt Caroline said. "We flew here in the helicopter, which is gone under piles of snow."

The Amber Giant thought for a minute, then grinned.

"I will carry all the humans down to Kathmandu," the Amber Giant said. "Then I will come back up here and help find caves."

"I will eat ice while I wait," the Ice Giant said and stared at her arms. "I have never been so thin!"

As the Ice Giant turned to go, she leaned towards Elika.

"Thank you for everything, Elika," she said. "I truly hope to see you again."

"Me too," Elika said, and she meant it.

"Do you think you can be friends with Amby?" Elika whispered so only the Ice Giant could hear.

"We'll see," the Ice Giant whispered back. "He's not like any giant I have met before. I want to learn all about him."

She leaned her massive head closer to Elika's small, human one.

"You didn't tell me about all his hair, though,"

the Ice Giant said even more quietly near her ear, which created a very cold breeze that tickled her.

Elika giggled. It was the first joke the Ice Giant ever told her.

The Amber Giant gathered the group of humans in his warm, furry hands. Even though it smelled, Elika was so glad to be in a warm place that she didn't mind. She didn't even feel scared to be in a giant's hand.

Aunt Caroline elbowed Elika.

"Didn't I tell you it would all be fine in the end?" Aunt Caroline said.

"Yes, and you said the craziest plans are the ones that work," Elika said. "I think you were right."

"You're getting the hang of this adventure business," Aunt Caroline said, and hugged her.

Elika held on to Amby's thumb and waved goodbye to the Ice Giant.

"Goodbye, Elika," the Ice Giant said. "Until we meet again."

Chapter
Twenty-three

A few weeks after Elika left the Himalayas, she was at home in her room in Hartsdale, New York. She lounged on her bed in a yellow summer dress. After her time in freezing places, she couldn't get enough of the heat.

It was Friday, her favorite day.

And to make it better, Aunt Caroline was coming to dinner.

Elika hopped down the stairs to help her mom set the table.

"How was swimming class today?" her mom asked. To make the most of the summer sunshine, Elika was taking lessons at the outdoor, public pool.

"It was good," Elika said. "Henry was there too."

"Ah, French Henry," her mom said with a knowing look in her eye. "So, are you learning more words?"

"Well, I kind of stopped learning French," Elika said.

"You did?" Elika's mom said as she carried a stack of plates to the table.

"Yeah, I wanted to surprise you," Elika said. "But since you brought it up, I'm learning Icelandic."

Her mom almost dropped the plates. Elika helped her put them carefully on the table.

"Wow," her mom said. "I am surprised."

"I found a free language site online," Elika said as she lay out forks and knives. "It's really good. I even record my voice and they have people in Iceland listen to the pronunciation. I am teaching Henry what I'm learning. He might try the site too."

"That's wonderful, Elika," her mom said. "Why did you change your mind about learning French?"

"It was the Ice Giant's idea," Elika said, as she folded a napkin for each plate setting. "She said I should learn the language of my own people."

A smile curled on her mom's face.

"Well, I agree with the Ice Giant," she said softly. "And anytime you want to practice with me, I would love to speak Icelandic with you."

"Takk," Elika said, which was Icelandic for thanks.

Her mom smiled bigger and said, *"Verði þér að góðu"*. Elika thought it meant 'you're welcome', but she wasn't quite sure. She was about to ask her mom to repeat it slowly when a knock sounded at the door.

Elika went to open it. When she saw Aunt Caroline, Elika gave her a big hug.

Aunt Caroline was just back from Nepal. She had stayed for a few weeks to help the giants get used to each other. Her face was red from the cold mountain air of the Himalayas, and her lips were very chapped. But she smiled happily.

"Nice dress, Elika," Aunt Caroline said, examining her. "It brings out your eyes."

"Yeah," Elika said. "I know."

Her mom, who came to greet Aunt Caroline, overheard them.

"You are actually wearing a color that brings out your eyes…on purpose?" her mom asked Elika.

"Well, I have strange eyes," Elika said. "But I think they are a good strange."

Her mom hugged her.

"I think they are a wonderful strange," her mom said.

Aunt Caroline sat at the table, and drank a tall glass of sparkling water. Elika sat across from her.

"So, tell me," Elika said. "Do the Ice Giant and the Amber Giant get along?"

Aunt Caroline had been with them in the mountains for three weeks. Hopefully she would have some good news for Elika.

"Well, they are very different," Aunt Caroline said. "And the Ice Giant is still not too fond of me, so I don't think she'd share her feelings. But she said to thank you and tell you she is glad she came to the mountains."

"Well, that's good," Elika said. "Is she OK with the sun and everything?" The sun was a lot stronger in Nepal compared with Iceland, which was a lot farther north.

"The Amber Giant collected leaves for her, and she has made a sun garment like the one she had in Iceland," Aunt Caroline said. "She wanted me to give you this."

Aunt Caroline passed her a little purse made

entirely of woven leaves. It looked very pretty, and when Elika examined it, she realized it was strong.

"Wow, it seems stronger than I would expect," Elika said.

"Me too," Aunt Caroline said. "The Ice Giant must have some tricks up her sleeve. She wouldn't tell me how she made it, of course."

Elika smiled. Maybe one day the Ice Giant would tell her, if they met again.

"So, Elika, have you been dreaming of the Ice Giant at all?" Aunt Caroline asked.

Elika shook her head. She slept well every night, without insomnia or bad dreams.

"I'm dream-free," Elika said and smiled.

Elika's mom lay a bread basket on the table. Aunt Caroline quickly ate two large pieces of sourdough and drank a second glass of water.

"You look like you could use some rest," Elika's mom said to Aunt Caroline. "How about we go for a facial, and a relaxing massage at the spa?"

Aunt Caroline nodded. "It would be great to have some moisturizer on this chapped face of mine!" she said. "But it will have to be soon. I'm only here for two weeks."

"Are you going back to Nepal so soon?" Elika's mom asked.

Aunt Caroline shook her head no.

"Are you going to Iceland?" Elika asked. "To find the Ice Giant's cave there?"

Aunt Caroline swallowed a bite of a third piece of bread. "Actually," she said, "I'm going to a conference on climate change in Bermuda. With Edmund." She blushed.

Elika and her mom exchanged looks. Did Aunt Caroline have a boyfriend?

"I'm so happy for you, Caroline," her mom said. "What's he like?"

"Oh, Edmund, he's…sweet," Aunt Caroline said, and stuffed another piece of bread into her mouth. Elika got the feeling she was embarrassed to talk about him.

"So, Mom," Elika said. "You thought finding the giant might change me? Well, I think it changed Aunt Caroline instead."

"Oh, I don't know," her mom said. "You seem different to me too."

Elika thought about how before she met the Ice Giant, she hadn't ever wanted to meet a giant. She studied the leaf purse. Now it seemed she was friends with one.

And she actually liked Aunt Caroline now.

Also, she was learning Icelandic.

"OK, I guess I'm different too," Elika said. "But I don't want to spend my life in the mountains camping in the snow, that's for sure."

Aunt Caroline laughed.

"You know, Elika, as much as I love the cold mountains, I'm kind of looking forward to a tropical destination for once," Aunt Caroline said.

"Yeah," Elika said. "But you never know what you might find in the Bermuda triangle."

Aunt Caroline looked nervous for a moment. Then she shrugged. "You can never have too many giants in the family..."

"Is that one of grandma's sayings?" Elika asked.

"Your grandma never knew about the Amber Giant," Aunt Caroline said. "She didn't believe in giants. Thought they were strange." She winked at Elika.

"Oh, giants are strange," Elika said. "But good strange."

"Like me?" Aunt Caroline said.

"Yes, like you," Elika said. "And me too. Because I love giants, just like everyone else in my weird family."

They laughed together.

Elika hoped that somewhere high in the Himalayas, the Amber Giant and the Ice Giant were laughing too.

About the
Author

Giulietta M. Spudich enjoys writing everything from children's stories to grown-up fiction, and poems in between. She lives in Cambridge, England where she moved from California in 2002. She is inspired by cats, especially her late black cat, Smokey.

Find Giulietta on Twitter @spudichpen.

Discover more at:
www.handersenpublishing.com

A special thank you to the kids and staff at Bluestem Montessori Elementary School for their fabulous feedback and wonderful art work.

Friendship can come in the most unlikely of places.

The Amber GIANT

Giulietta M. Spudich

Discover the story of
The Amber Giant

Thank you for purchasing and reading *The Ice Giant*.

Handersen Publishing is an independent publishing house that specializes in creating quality young adult, middle grade, and picture books.

We hope you enjoyed this book and will consider leaving a review on Amazon or Goodreads. A small review can make a big difference.

Thank you.

Handersen Publishing LLC
Great books for young readers
www.handersenpublishing.com

Lightning Source UK Ltd.
Milton Keynes UK
UKHW041155090219
336887UK00001B/63/P